"Zeischegg pulls you into a bleeding-edge now shot through with a perverse, polymorphous, and evolving fear. The victims trust nothing, pity nothing, see their own lives through sliding glass—and resolutely refuse to stay innocent."

—**ZAK SMITH,** author of *Pictures Showing What Happens on Each Page of Thomas Pynchon's Novel Gravity's Rainbow*

"Raw, startling, and haunting, this book is truly unforgettable. Chris Zeischegg is a gifted storyteller, unafraid to explore the darkest recesses of identity, desire, power, and pleasure."

—**TRISTAN TAORMINO**, author of *The Ultimate Guide to Kink*

"Christopher Zeischegg has a knack for obscuring his autobiography with genre, blurring the lines between fiction and reality like he blurs the lines between Chris and Danny Wylde. Intercut between the suspense and the horror are genuine reflections on the experiences of a queer man in a straight industry and the struggle of sexual beings in a conservative world."

—**JOHNNY MURDOC,** publisher, Queer Young Cowboys

"This is a journey of self-exploration and self-exploitation I don't remember reading before. This is a new author figuring out what makes him tick. The further he explores, the better it gets, and the traces of young Gregg Araki and Dennis Cooper I sense within the writing could well bloom into something extraordinary."

—**ALES KOT**

THE WOLVES THAT LIVE IN SKIN AND SPACE

A NOVEL

THE WOLVES THAT LIVE IN SKIN AND SPACE

CHRISTOPHER ZEISCHEGG
AKA DANNY WYLDE

BARNACLE | RARE BIRD

THIS IS A GENUINE BARNACLE BOOK

A Barnacle Book | Rare Bird Books
453 South Spring Street, Suite 302
Los Angeles, CA 90013
rarebirdbooks.com

Set in Minion
Printed in the United States

10 9 8 7 6 5 4 3 2 1

Publisher's Cataloging-in-Publication data

Zeischegg, Christopher.
    The Wolves that live in skin and space / by Christopher Zeischegg ,
aka Danny Wylde.
    p. cm.
    ISBN 9781940207773

1. Wylde, Danny—Fiction. 2. Pornography—Fiction. 3. Sex-oriented
businesses—Fiction. 4. Gay men—Fiction. 5. Homosexuality—Fiction.
6. Los Angeles (Calif.)—Fiction. 7. Gothic fiction. 8. Horror fiction. I.
Title.

PS3626.E353 .W65 2015

813.6—dc23

To the adult industry.
You've been my lover and enemy, and will be neither again.

ALSO BY CHRISTOPHER ZEISCHEGG

Come to my Brother

1.

He often waits up to three minutes once I log in. But tonight's call comes quick. Within seconds. He's set a new record.

There's breathing, panting even. It means he's leaned up close to his mic. Or scared. "Are you there?"

"Yeah," I say. "What's up, Damien?"

"Do you think you can come on cam?" he asks. "I really need to talk to you."

"Hold on." I position my webcam to show my face and upper body. Then I take off my shirt. "Okay. Can you see me?"

"Yeah." His image pops up on my screen. Like usual, he swivels back and forth in a black office chair. "First, I want to let you know that I didn't mean for this to happen. It just did. I'm so sorry."

"Is something wrong?"

"No," says Damien. Then, "Maybe. It's just that..."

I smile and tell him, "It's okay."

"How do I say this?"

"I don't know," I answer. "You should probably just tell me."

"It's just that..."

"That bad, huh?"

"No," he says. "Okay. I didn't mean for it to happen. But I think I'm in love with you." The swiveling stops. There's silence. The breathing is gone, and I mean mine too. "You look upset.

Tell me exactly what you're thinking. I don't want you to be upset."

"I'm not upset, Damien. I think…" I'm trying to decide if I still want his money. "Maybe you're being unrealistic."

"I know we're just friends, and I don't expect it to turn into anything else."

"Can I ask you a serious question?"

"You're not even looking at me," says Damien. "Can we forget that I said anything?"

"Do you pay any of your other friends to talk to you?"

"No," he answers. "But I don't think of it like I'm paying you. I'm helping you out. Because I want to."

"But you're, like, my age," I tell him. "You should spend your money on something useful, or fun."

"I think that maybe I didn't use the right word. Maybe it's not really love. It's just that you haven't been online much, and I've had some bad days at work. I was thinking about how much better it would be if I was in LA with you, and not here." He stops for a moment. "Do you know what I mean?"

"Listen, I have to go."

"Can we talk about this? Please?"

"Maybe later. I'm kind of tired," I lie.

"But you just got online."

"I know."

"What if I pay you more?" he asks.

I pause too long, which means I'm considering it.

"How long would you be able to stay?" He's made an assumption, and he's right. I'm unbuttoning my pants.

"About an hour."

"You can't stay any longer?"

"An hour," I say, like I'm standing my ground. Then I grasp my cock and work it up to a semi-erect state.

"You don't have to do that," he says. "If you don't want to."

"You don't like it?"

"No, I like it," he tells me. "But it's not a show, right? You'd be doing it anyway?"

My eyes are closed. I say, "Mhmm," and think about a dream I had a long time ago.

Damien talks about his day at work and deposits money into my PayPal account.

2.

I'VE DIVIDED MY INCOME INTO three separate categories. Or it's divided itself. I just designate where it goes. Doing scenes pays for rent, utilities, clothing, and necessities. Except for food. I pay for groceries with the money I make from camming.

Damien is a separate category altogether. He's my most regular client, and different in the fact that he never jerks off to me. He just talks about his day, or week, or whatever. I spend his money on toys.

Porno lights the stove top. Camming provides the stuff to throw in the pot. Damien lets me browse the eBay listings while I eat my meal. He affords me two fifteen-inch DJ speakers and a 1000-watt amplifier.

The speakers aren't all superfluous. I've been trying to start a band for about a year. It's been a slow process because drummers are hard to come by in LA. At least good ones. They exist, but mostly as studio musicians and hire-ons for touring bands. I've bypassed the issue and started programming electronic beats on my laptop. I just need them to be louder.

My friend, Thad, already plays bass and has been messing around with a microKORG synthesizer. There's a guy I met through work who wants to do vocals. I play guitar. With my laptop and speakers, we're a full band.

3.

"IT'S DANCEABLE. REALLY DARK AND gothy," says Thad. "I'm into it."

We've borrowed our friends' practice space to see if we're capable of writing music together. From the sound of it, we are. Thad throws down distorted synth tracks and I riff on some guitar parts I've already come up with. The vocalist, Mario, sits on the floor with his notepad open. He nods back and forth to the beat. His lips move but nothing comes out. I think he's working it out in his head.

"Do you think it would be cool if I did some backup vocals here?" I ask. "Like black metal-style screaming?"

"Yeah, I like that idea," says Mario.

"I just don't know what to say," I tell him. "If you give me something to say..."

He tries to explain the song. It's about religion, or the government. "That's what's cool about it," he says. "You can interpret it a bunch of different ways."

I've forgotten the line by the time we're back into the song. I just scream what sounds good in my head. It's more of a syllabic noise than an actual word. No one can tell the difference.

Our attempts to move on fail because my guitar amp suddenly cuts out. The light on the power switch is still on. It's buzzing. None of us know much about amplifiers, so we can't figure out what's wrong.

"Let us know when you get it fixed," says Thad. "'cause that was fun."

4.

My friend, Sara, invites me to dinner at her place. I arrive late. No one's eating or even seated at the table.

"You met Victor and Allejandra at my Halloween party," says Sara, introducing me to her other guests.

"I was the killer clown," says Victor as we shake hands.

"I think I was a piece of fruit, or a vegetable," I say. "It's nice to meet you again."

Allejandra is Victor's wife. She's dressed in a slutty-looking schoolgirl outfit. Sara wears an exact replica. In a way, it still feels like Halloween.

"She got these in the mail today," says Allejandra. I think she's referring to Sara because there's no one else here.

"From a fan," adds Sara. "We're going to use them in my next video."

"Cute," I say, and I'm serious.

Something in the kitchen beeps. Minutes later, we're eating Shepherd's Pie.

"Every time I see her mother," says Victor, "she tells me, 'You should be a better example for my daughter. Why don't you set her on a righteous path?' I keep trying to tell her, 'I met your daughter because she was on the *wrong* path. That's where I want her to stay. It's why I love her.'" Allejandra laughs along with him.

"She knows what you do?" I ask Allejandra.

"Yes," she answers. "And she keeps dreaming. As if, at this point in my life, I'll start over as a nurse."

"You guys are basically the happiest couple ever," says Sara. "If I was your mother, I'd be proud."

"You're right." Allejandra squeezes Victor's hand. "When we first got together, I kept waiting for him to get mad at me. I was like, 'Come on. When are we gonna fight?'" Victor looks into her eyes and smiles. If they were strangers, it would be disgusting.

-

Sara glances at me, which could mean a number of things. I shift my eyes, smile, and brush her leg. Almost on accident. It's my interpretation of giving mixed signals.

After dinner, we sit in the living room and drink wine. Sara smokes some pot.

"So the schoolgirl thing is girl/girl only, right?" I ask.

"It's all I do," says Allejandra. "Sorry."

"I might use the costumes again for my site," adds Sara. This is relevant because she still fucks boys on camera.

"That's, um…" For lack of a better word, I say, "Cool."

"You two have worked together?" asks Victor. He motions to Sara and I.

"Once," I say.

"And?" Allejandra's mouth forms the shape of a laugh, but it doesn't follow through.

"I was worried," says Sara. "Because everyone told me he was going to be so submissive. I don't know why. That's obviously not the case."

"It was fun," I add.

"If I can get it together," says Sara, "the video should go up next week."

Victor pulls his phone out of his pocket and nearly spills his glass. "The time, it's uh…We should be going."

"You're driving?"

"No, no," says Victor. "I still need my license, babe."

"I don't?" Allejandra mocks resentment.

"See, we never fight." Victor leans down to give Sara a hug. Then he shakes my hand. Allejandra kisses me on the cheek. "Adios!"

I start looking for my shoes, and gather myself together.

"You're leaving, too?" Sara isn't giving me puppy dog eyes, but they're close.

"Oh. Yeah," I say. "I've got to work in the morning."

"Oh."

"Thanks, though. I had fun."

"Yeah, me too."

5.

BACK AT HOME, I CAN'T fall asleep. Something pulls at my brain like a tide stuck between it's ebb and flow. I'm reminded of the moon; its gravitational hold a likely culprit. When I step outside, all I see is city lights and blackened sky.

I turn my bedroom light on, and wish my apartment to appear like a star to some hovering astronaut. The same layer of smog that shields me from the moon probably blankets my home like tar. To the rest of the universe, I'm as bright as dark matter.

With thoughts like these, my only assurance of sleep is masturbation. I open my laptop and look for pictures of Sara on free porn sites. Then I log into my cam site and wait for lurking customers. A screen name pops up that I don't recognize: *TheWolf*.

"Hey babe," I say into the webcam. "Where you from?"

TheWolf: LA.

"Me too. What're you doing up so late?" I bite my lip, which I hope looks slutty enough to bypass the initial bullshit. I want to come and go to bed.

TheWolf: What do you think?

"You want to play? Click 'private' and I'm all yours."

TheWolf: Can you stand up first?

"Anything you want." I stand and jut my ass out towards the webcam.

A tinny bell rings from my laptop speakers. The screen reads, "*TheWolf* has requested a private chat." Digital cash flows at several dollars per minute.

"You like to suck cock? Or you'd rather fuck me?" I ask. There's no response, so I improvise. "I want you to get down on your knees, you fuckin' come slut. Open your mouth, babe. Yeah, just like that." I show a close-up of my cock while stroking it. Then I tell the stranger to shove it down his throat.

There's no response. So I keep blabbering, "Fuck," and, "I love your fucking mouth," while I browse pictures of Sara in a separate window. She keeps my dick hard. My imagination helps.

Fifteen minutes in, I ask, "Are you gonna come with me?"

The Wolf: Would you be interested in meeting up?

The Wolf: In real life?

I stop jerking off. "Um, I don't really do that. Sorry."

The Wolf: I'd make it worth your while.

"Yeah?" I sort of laugh. "What's worth my while?"

The Wolf: Maybe $2000.

My eyes grow wide. "Just to meet up?"

The Wolf: No.

"Listen, that's really generous of you," I say. "But I'm not, you know, a hustler or anything. It's a different kind of gig."

The Wolf: Think about it.

"Okay. I will," I tell him. "Do you still want me to come?"

The Wolf: Yes.

6.

OATMEAL. PROTEIN SHAKE. SHOWER. A bus ride to the downtown warehouse district.

The location is in the second story of an old brick building. Once inside, it looks like a middle-class apartment.

"Danny, what's up?" asks the cameraman. He grabs my palm and leans in.

"You know, whatever. I'm good."

"Good."

"You?" I ask.

"Should I tell him about our day?" he shouts back to the director. There's a mumbled response. It's more of a shrug.

"Why, what happened?"

I'm told the first performer couldn't get his dick hard and the second girl canceled. It's been six hours on set with nothing accomplished. "So don't fuck this up," says the cameraman. "Without a scene, we're just doing this for free."

I peek around him. There's a girl applying makeup on the other side of the room.

"Look at that ass," says the cameraman. "If that's a problem for you, you're fuckin'...I don't know, man."

"Have I ever been a problem?"

"I know you got this. Just been one of those days." He slams a pen down on a thin stack of paper. "Do your thing."

I skim the paperwork and sign my name a half dozen times. The girl walks over.

"Hey, I'm Danny," I tell her.

She smiles. "Rose."

"You've been doing this for long?" I ask.

"About a year, on and off. You?"

"I don't know."

"You don't know?" She looks confused.

"A couple years," I say, to which Rose nods her head.

Thirty minutes later, I'm buried in her ass. My fist is wrapped around a tuft of her hair. Our communication still rests on a few choice words. "Fuck. Oh my god. Oh my god." The rest passes through our skin.

7.

I TAKE A BUS TO Hollywood before I head home. There's a Guitar Center and I want to see about getting my amp fixed. Inside, I'm hit with *déjà vu*. The orchestration is always the same. Every scale is played at once. A boy tries out his first guitar. There's a keyboard DJ, an electric shredder, some acoustic god, and a kid in the back with an erratic kick drum. The noise should be dense and moving. An amalgamation of warring notes sound ripe for emerging patterns. But none of us can quite put it together. So it's just a bunch of shit that makes me feel old and want to say, "Keep it down," or buy something louder to drown it all out. When I think about it, that's really the point of this place. I tell the first customer service representative I see, "Good job."

He misunderstands me and asks if he can help. I talk about my amplifier as if it's broken. Then the guy says, "Great," and points me in the direction of new ones. I don't explain or argue with him. My face probably does something like cringe, because everything he shows me costs a lot of money.

I get a text message and pretend it's a phone call. So I talk to myself for a few minutes and the customer service guy goes away.

When I actually look at my phone, I see the text is from Sara: *I keep having dreams about u.* That's when I decide to leave.

8.

AT HOME, I LOG ON to Skype. Damien tries to message me. I see that Sara is online, so I block Damien and type to her instead.

Danny: Any of them nightmares?

She responds with a request for video chat. I accept and Sara's image comes to life in amazing low-resolution.

I say, "Hey," and so does she.

"How was, um, work?"

"It was typical."

"If things weren't so typical…" She pauses. "I don't know. Do you think you'd have spent the night?"

"That's a pretty loaded question," I tell her.

"Okay," she says. "I get it. You don't want to fuck me. I guess I'll get over it. Still feels kind of shitty, you know? The rejection, or whatever you want to call it."

"I don't think it has much to do with wanting to fuck you or not," I say.

"I know. It's work, and being jaded and stuff, right?"

"What do you mean?"

"Jared got drunk the other night and told me how he doesn't even like having sex with his girlfriend anymore. He works all the time. Sometimes two scenes a day. The last thing he wants to do at home is fuck."

"It's not that I hate sex. It's still fun. But yeah…"

"So you're like Jared?" she asks, or just concludes.

"There's only so many times I can come in a day, and with the camming thing, too…It's just, like, I need the money." I look directly into the webcam. "You're totally cute, Sara. You know that."

"I don't think 'cute' is what I'm going for. But thanks."

"I think it's cool I'm in your dreams," I tell her.

"You're so fucking…I don't know," she says.

"Can I ask what happened in them? In your dreams?"

"No," she says. "At this point, it would be way too masochistic. Even for me."

"I still jerk off to your pictures. Does that make you feel better?"

She laughs in a way that seems authentic. "Always, Danny. I guess that's the best compliment I'm gonna get."

"You're beautiful and I think we should go see a movie or something," I say.

"Give me a few days to wallow."

"Of course."

"You realize," she says, "there's actually nothing special about you."

"I'm aware of that," I mutter, like it's an ingrained response. Suddenly, it becomes a big deal that I've said this. I kiss Sara goodbye, digitally, and think about why.

9.

WHEN I'M THINKING, WHICH MEANS listening to repetitive music and drinking canned coconut water and staring at the wall, I get a message from *TheWolf*. It's strange because I don't remember logging in to the cam site.

TheWolf: Have you given it some thought?

Danny: Yes.

TheWolf: Your cam is on.

"Oh," I say. "I didn't know. But yes, I've thought about it."

TheWolf: I suggest that we meet tomorrow. In public. Just to talk. You will see that I'm okay.

He sends me the address for a coffee shop less than a mile from my apartment. It freaks me out that he's so close by. I lie and tell him, "That's on the other side of town."

TheWolf: If you'd rather meet somewhere else, say so.

"No," I tell him. "There's nowhere else. But you only asked if I thought about it. I haven't come to a conclusion."

TheWolf: I will be there tomorrow. 2:00 p.m. I think you should come.

"Okay. Well, I have to go."

TheWolf: I will give you something just for meeting me.

"Yeah, that's cool," I say. "I guess we'll see, right?" I try to laugh. "Sweet dreams." My hand does one of those Jackie Onassis waves.

TheWolf: I look forward to meeting you.

10.

THE MAILMAN COMES IN THE morning and knocks on my door. "I need you to sign for this," he says.

The package is from Damien. It's weird because I don't remember giving him my address. But there's an iPod inside, so I'm not that pissed about it.

I unblock Damien on Skype, and say, "Thank you."

"You got my package?"

"Yeah. That was really cool of you."

"I know you like music," he stammers. "And I thought that would be the best gift for someone who likes music."

"Believe it or not," I say, "I've gone all this time without an iPod. It's perfect. Thank you."

"I'm so happy," he replies. "I was scared that you might have had the same one."

"Listen, I love the iPod, and I'm not really upset, but how did you get my address?"

"Oh." He looks away. "You're not mad, right?"

"Like I said."

"You post your real name on Facebook. Or your friends do."

"They don't post my address."

"I know, but it's not that hard to find with the Internet and everything," says Damien. "Please don't be mad at me. I wanted it to be a surprise."

"It was a very nice surprise."

"How long can you talk?" he asks.

"I actually have a meeting in a little bit," I tell him.

"So how long?"

"I have to go to the meeting right now," I insist.

"Not even a couple minutes? I need to talk about the other night."

I block him once more and rub my eyes like I have a headache, which I anticipate but don't actually feel. Then I hear a noise from my laptop and realize that Thad's trying to video chat with me.

"You there, dude?"

I turn my webcam back on and say, "Yes. Look at me. I'm here."

"What's up with your amp?" asks Thad.

"I went to Guitar Center. It seems like it would cost a lot of money."

"Bummer. You're not gonna fix it?"

"I will," I tell him. "Soon. I just have to come up with the money."

"Okay. Check this out though." He shifts his webcam to a view of his microKORG synthesizer. One of the drum tracks I programmed starts playing in the background. Thad hits some keys and gets really into it. I watch him play along to the whole song.

My lack of participation is awful. I imagine it's what parents feel like when they give their kid up for adoption. The adopted parents send video tapes of the kid, like, "Here's your fucking brat. I'm raising him to hate you." Except much less devastating. Because I like Thad, and the song's not all that personal.

But I hate that I don't have a choice in the matter. I can't add to my own creation without some sort of noise machine.

It feels like Thad's said something I didn't pay attention to. "Could you use that amp you bought for the DJ speakers?" he asks later. "In the meantime?"

"I guess, but then we couldn't hear the drums," I tell him.

"Right."

"I could probably get the money if I did something weird."

"Like what?" he asks.

"I don't know yet. I could probably find out later today."

"That sounds cryptic, dude," says Thad. "And I'm all about that. I say, 'Do it.'"

11.

I'M AT THE COFFEE SHOP waiting for *The Wolf* and listening to Crystal Castles on my new iPod. It's ten past two, and the guy's not here yet. It occurs to me that the whole thing's a joke. Five minutes go by and I'm convinced *The Wolf* doesn't even live in LA.

The coffee here is good and I always have a lot of time to waste. So it's not like I feel stupid for sitting in a coffee shop by myself. I feel stupid for thinking about the money and for pretending it was real. Most of my hooker friends don't make two grand a john.

I walk home listening to Alice Glass singing, "We were lovers / Now we can't be friends," and think about how her terminology's all fucked up. *A lover is just someone who feels something profound after getting fucked, and doesn't know what to call it.* For a while, he thinks it has something to do with another person. Then he gets bored with everything that person does outside of sex. Then he gets bored with the sex. That's not really love. Otherwise, he'd stay with that person forever, which doesn't happen anymore.

An old man with an oxygen-tank-on-wheels looks at me before I cross the street to my apartment. I give him the finger because that's how I feel.

12.

A NAP IS IN ORDER, but I get distracted by a knock at the door. I open it and find myself standing alone. Except for a package. It joins me at my feet.

The mailman's already come today and there's no address on the package. I start having one of those 9-11 moments because it could be a bomb, or anthrax, or something. Then I feel like I'm not important enough to kill in that prolific kind of way. So I just open the package.

With the bubble wrap gone, I'm left holding a piece of thick, red fabric. It unfolds into something larger: an article of clothing maybe. Laid out on my bed, it looks like a dress or robe. But it has a hood, so it's kind of like a sweatshirt, too.

I take another shower, because I feel like starting the day over. Then I sit at my computer because I don't know what else to do.

The red thing is still on my bed. It makes me uncomfortable. I had hoped it was part of my imagination. Now I have to confront it and figure out what it means.

My laptop is open and I'm logged into the cam site. I'm almost sure that I didn't do this, because I haven't touched my computer since this morning. What's worse: *The Wolf* is the only screen name lurking in my free chat room. He hasn't typed a thing.

I'm waiting for *The Wolf* and *The Wolf* is waiting for me. That's what I believe: that we're having this standoff.

Finally, I give in. "Hey…"

The Wolf: Did you get my package?

"Oh, I get it. You're fucking with me," I say. "How about I call the police?"

The Wolf: Gifting is not a crime.

"Where were you today?" I ask.

The Wolf: At the coffee shop.

"I was at the coffee shop."

The Wolf: I know.

"Fuck you," I tell him. "You followed me home?"

The Wolf: I looked at you while walking.

"This is a fucking invasion of privacy," I shout at my laptop. "You're a piece of shit, you know that?"

The Wolf: You have something important to do.

The Wolf: I'm willing to pay you for it.

"Oh my god, I'm blocking you."

The Wolf: Don't you want to know about the red riding hood?

"That thing?" I look to the fabric on my bed. "I'm not a fucking girl, dude. I don't wear dresses."

The Wolf: Come over.

He types out an address that is probably not far from here.

TheWolf: And wear your red riding hood.

"You're blocked." I click a button and prevent him from contacting me again.

13.

I'VE LOCKED MY DOOR, CRAWLED under my covers, and laid there for some time. It's only a quarter-to-four, but the day's been way too much to deal with.

I remember that I haven't eaten, and it might be why I'm so tired. The fridge is empty except for condiments and canned coconut water. I might have to go outside. Hunt and scavenge. Maybe pay for food.

I peek through the blinds to see if anyone's outside. People are milling about. I'm just worried about one of them. But I have no idea what *TheWolf* looks like. No one's wearing matted fur or other canine paraphernalia. At least that I can see.

The door opens, closes, and then locks shut. I'm outside on a set of stairs. It feels like a big step, metaphorically speaking. A flood of courage rushes through my veins. After that, a drought.

There's a sound like the crack of a whip. The air parts before me. A piece of window shatters near the front door. Seconds later, someone on the sidewalk falls to the ground. A red mist hovers over her body.

I can hear a distant scream when I fumble for the lock. My key presses against it like a virgin boy. Eventually something clicks and I fling myself forward.

When I stop shaking, I'm on the apartment floor. My palms are plastered to my ears and my fingers to my scalp. Everything is quiet.

I feel like I should do something, but I can't keep from staring at the hole in my refrigerator door. The opening looks wide enough to stick my finger through.

Inside the refrigerator, things are a mess. A ketchup bottle has exploded. There is glass and tomato paste everywhere. I finger a bullet from what could have been my lunch. It's still warm.

The most appropriate thing I can think of is to call the police. That's what I try to do. I'm dialing 911 when my phone is shot from my grasp. Whoever's out there is really fucking good with a gun.

14.

I'm on Skype and telling Sara, "You have to call the police. Someone's outside, like, fucking shooting at my apartment."

"You mean filming you?" she asks.

"No," I whisper harshly. "Shooting with a gun." I hold the bullet up to the webcam. "See?"

She looks skeptical. "Why don't you call the police?"

"Because my phone has a fucking hole in it. Anyway, I think I know who it is. It's this creep from the Internet."

"You're serious? Someone's shooting at you?"

"Yes. Right now. Please call the police."

"I don't hear any shooting," she says.

"Fuck. How do you want me to convince you? Should I go stand by the window and get shot? You want to see blood or something?"

"Okay," says Sara. "I guess I believe you. It's just that you don't seem all that scared. I'm trying to read you, and it doesn't seem like you're in immediate danger. You know, 'cause you're on Skype."

I smile, briefly, because the situation is absurd. "I'm on Skype because I want you to call the police."

"See, you're laughing."

"No, I'm not," I insist. Then I realize she's right. "Well, yeah, because this is fucking, like, whatever…It's insane that I'm having this conversation with you."

"How about I just come over?" She suggests.

"No. Listen, I don't want you to get shot either."

"You realize I could get in a lot of trouble for calling the cops," she says.

"Why would you get in trouble?"

"I mean, if you're lying, or joking, or whatever."

The conversation turns to something futile.

"Okay," she continues. "I'm trying to logically figure this out. If someone fired a gun, the cops would probably be there by now. Or they'd be really close. Or someone in your neighborhood would have at least called them. Right?"

"I don't know. It wasn't that loud." I'm staring at the screen. It's becoming one big blur.

"So it was a quiet gunshot…"

"They could have used a silencer," I suggest. "Sara, you're not being helpful. And I wish… I mean, if you're not gonna call the cops, I have to go."

"Now I can't tell if you're being serious."

I end the video chat and sit for several minutes. It's become altogether obvious that I can't be taken seriously. And that's profound in its own special—or unspecial—way.

15.

It's a big decision, but I log back on to the cam site and unblock *TheWolf*. His screen name pops up instantly.

TheWolf: I told you to wear your red riding hood.

Another name enters the chat room: *HardStud35*.

HardStud35: Hey. 35/GE/BH/8" here. What are you packing?

"The cops will be here soon," I say to *TheWolf*. "You're fucked."

TheWolf: They're here already. Look out your window.

HardStud35: You're cute, beau. But crazy!!! LOL.

I try to call his bluff. "If I go to the window, you'll shoot me."

TheWolf: No. But talk to the police and I will.

HardStud35: Um, I'll shoot my load if you stay.

I turn off my webcam and rush to the bathroom. A mirrored cabinet sits above the sink. I smash it and break off a piece of splintered glass. Then I tape it to a pencil and crawl towards the window near my front door.

I sit beneath the windowsill and twirl the makeshift device between my fingers. It reflects an image of the outside world. There's a squad car parked on the street below and I can see a part of an ambulance. Two paramedics hoist someone on to a stretcher.

Back at my computer, I scoff at *TheWolf*. "You'll be in handcuffs before the hour's through. All I have to do is wait."

There's no response.

"My uncle's a fuckin' lawyer," I say. "Seriously, you're fucked."

HardStud35: I don't get it. Do you want to go private or not?

It occurs to me that *TheWolf* might have already been caught. The police wouldn't bother to log him off the website. They'd just tackle him to the floor, stick a boot to the back of his neck, and rough him up a bit. Because they're the LAPD and that's part of the job description.

HardStud35: ???

"Hard stud… This is, um, not the best time."

16.

IT'S BEEN HOURS AND I'VE been asleep. Or I've been pretending. I feel that if I stay still long enough, I'll figure out that I'm in a dream and wake up somewhere else. It's not really working, and now I'm awake. Someone's knocking at the door.

My heart thumps as I crawl towards the window. I use the piece of mirror to look outside. This time it reflects the image of a person standing near my door. It's Sara and she looks almost worried.

I let her inside. "This way," I motion with my hands. "Quickly."

She pauses, looks over her shoulder, and then shuffles towards me with some improvised gusto.

"Are you okay?"

I lead her to my bedroom where I finally stop crouching and sit on my bed. "Well, you're alive. And I'm alive."

She plops down beside me, but leaves a big enough gap to convey a sort of physical metaphor. At least that's how I take it. "It occurred to me that…" She starts over. "First of all, I should probably say, 'I'm sorry.' Then again, I'm confused."

"About what?" I ask.

"Should I be sorry?"

"If it's for not calling the police, I don't know." I think about scratching my scalp while doing it, which makes me feel self-conscious about having a nervous twitch, or faking one. "They seem to have already done their job."

"It really happened?"

"Yeah. Someone shot my refrigerator."

Sara lets out a deep breath. Then she leans over and hugs me. "Danny, I'm so sorry. I feel like an asshole."

"And my window. I have to get a new window."

She rests her head on my shoulder. "But you're safe, right? They caught him?"

"The police showed up, but I don't know," I say. "I think someone died."

"What do you mean?"

"I saw someone get shot."

Sara squeezes harder. "Jesus. Maybe you should think about moving. I could rent you a room. I'll even let you stay for free for a while…if that's what you need." When I don't respond, she adds, "I'm not trying to be weird or anything. I promise."

I rest my head on hers. "It's not really the neighborhood though."

"Well, statistically speaking…"

"No. I mean… I know who it was."

"You know the guy who shot at you?" she asks.

"Not personally," I tell her. "But I've jerked off for him on the Internet. He wanted to meet in real life. I thought I could make some extra money, you know?"

"Danny, that's really dangerous," she says. Then, "You're not making enough money?"

"Enough for all this, I guess." I'm looking around my apartment, so I hope she knows what I mean. "Don't you escort sometimes?"

"I used to," she admits. "But not with guys I met on the Internet. I know I'm not one to talk. Just be careful, okay?"

We're both sitting up. No longer touching each other.

"You're pissed at me now?" she asks.

"No," I say, truthfully. "It's cool you came over. I'm just hungry and afraid to go outside."

"Let's order some food. We don't have to go anywhere."

"Yeah, that sounds good," I say. "Can you make the decision though?"

"About what?" she asks.

"Like, what kind of food, or where to get it." My voice is getting softer. "I don't think I'm good at making decisions right now."

"Okay," she says.

17.

WE EAT OUT OF STYROFOAM cartons. The food is greasy and Asian, which is about as comforting as it gets. Plus, Sara's ordered these little bottles of sake, and we've emptied most of them into our cups and mouths. Things don't feel as terrifying.

Sara smiles and says, "You look like a dog right now."

I can't talk because noodles are falling out of my mouth. I try to say, "What?"

"That came out wrong." She laughs. "But you've seen *Lady and the Tramp?* The cartoon with the dogs?"

"Oh yeah," I tell her. "The part with the noodles. I look nothing like that."

"That was my idea of romance when I was—maybe—five," says Sara. "Now I just want to feel like a knight in shining armor, or a tramp in shining armor. I know I didn't save you from anything, but you're smiling now and you weren't earlier."

"I'll give you that," I say. "You kind of saved the day."

"Wow," she says, rolling her eyes back into her head. "You almost die and I turn it into something about me."

"I don't want to think about dying, so this is, like, really cool, babe."

"Did you just call me 'babe?'" There's another one of her laughs.

"It's what I call people on cam because it seems like the most typical pet name. It doesn't seem that personal, and it won't offend anyone. But it still sounds nice."

"Maybe when your dick is out," says Sara. "But I'm not on cam. And…"

"I know, I know. It's become a habit."

"You should talk to more people in real life," she says.

"I read somewhere that the primary form of communication for people under eighteen is texting. With camming, I still use my mouth."

"You're a rebel, aren't you?"

"My mouth is a weapon," I say. "So yes? I'm the Che Guevara of sitting at my desk."

Sara shuts up and takes a couple bites of Szechwan shrimp.

"Listen, that thing you said the other day...maybe it was yesterday..." I draw a blank because I've noticed Sara's eyes staring somewhere near my crotch. Then I notice it's because I'm sort of grabbing my cock through my pants. It's another habit I quickly take note of, and stop. "You said there's nothing interesting about me."

"Did I?"

"Yeah. I think so. Maybe you used a different word."

"When was this?" she asks.

"We were on Skype. It was the last thing you said before I logged off."

"I was probably just upset," she says.

"Oh."

"You can't take everything I say seriously when I'm suffering." Sara rolls on to her back. "Like right now, 'cause this food is fucking me up."

"I didn't disagree with you, though. And I wanted to know if you had a reason, so I could kind of figure it out myself."

"There's no reason...other than what I said." Sara's closed her eyes, but she's obviously not asleep.

"Okay, but I've been thinking about this a lot. When someone on cam recognizes me from a movie, they usually get really excited. Maybe it's because I'm naked. But they've seen me naked before, and a Google search will bring up, like, a thousand naked pictures. So I don't think that's it."

"You were a fantasy, and now you're talking to them," says Sara. "I doubt it's more complicated than that."

"But I'm a fantasy for really stupid reasons. There's nothing interesting about it."

"What do you mean? We have sex. Everyone's interested in sex. If you have sex for a living, it's the only job every person will be interested in. If you're an architect, people have to be into architecture or something. Otherwise, who gives a shit?"

"But that's what I mean," I tell her. "Everyone can have sex. When you break it down, there's nothing interesting about it."

"You mean different."

"What?"

"You're afraid you're not different enough, right? That's not the same as being interesting."

I think about this for a minute. "But…"

"Look," Sara interrupts. "Do you think I'm interesting?"

"Well…"

"Oh god." She laughs. "I shouldn't have asked."

"No, I mean, yeah, I think you're interesting."

"Give me some reasons why."

"Um," I start off, "you're cute, and have good taste in music, and I think you've read more books than me. And I like your tattoos."

She sits up and stares at me. The look on her face is something I've never seen before. "Okay."

"Is that not good enough?"

"I don't know. It proves my point, though. How many other people do you know with tattoos and good taste in music?"

"I said you're cute, too."

"And read books," she says. "I heard you."

"I get what you mean," I say. "But in my defense, I would say there's, like, an intangible quality about you."

"When I'm getting fucked, no one cares about my intangible quality," she says. "When someone jerks off to you, they don't either."

"Maybe it's because I don't have one."

"No," She's getting upset. "Who cares? You want everyone who jerks off to you to…what? Get you?"

"It's something I've been thinking about."

"I have to pee." Sara stands up and knocks over the last bottle of sake. It pours into her purse. "Oh shit." She starts dumping out her belongings on to my carpet. "Fucking fuck." The phone in her hand doesn't do anything when she presses at it.

I get up and start moving towards the kitchen.

"Where are you going?" she asks me.
"To find some paper towels."

18.

WHEN I GET BACK, SARA's in the bathroom and her stuff is on the floor. I try to soak up the sake with some paper towels. The result looks like crippled origami.

"I have to go," says Sara once she's back in the room.

"Maybe you're drunk," I tell her. "Because I'm kind of drunk."

"I still have to go." She starts to pick up her things and blow on them.

"You can spend the night if you want. It's not a big deal."

"I have to make a phone call and I don't have a phone," she says. "And you don't have a phone."

"You don't think it can wait? I mean, it's pretty late."

She seems to think about this. "I could probably send an email."

"Use my computer." I make a motion with my hand to designate the obvious location.

Sara drops her things back on the wet carpet. Then she sits at my desk and brings my laptop to life. "Who's the wolf?" she asks. When I don't respond, she looks at me and goes, "What's wrong?"

I can see the laptop screen from here. The same few words are repeated several dozen times.

The Wolf: I'm still here.
The Wolf: I'm still here.
The Wolf: I'm still here.

19.

I'M BACK IN BED, TRYING again to close my eyes and wake up somewhere else. It's my second attempt. I could be insane for expecting different results. The fact that I'm aware of it suggests I'm trying too hard. Or I believe a gunshot to the face might feel less catastrophic if my mind is completely fucked.

My brain's still working though, because I'm coming up with other explanations for my behavior. Like the fact that my bed is lower than my window. If someone outside wants to shoot me, I'm almost bulletproof.

"Seriously, Danny, what the fuck are you doing?" asks Sara. She's crawled up on the bed with me and is hovering over my body.

"How upset are you about your phone? Because you might get more upset about this."

"You're the one who's making me upset," she says. "I don't know what you're doing."

"I think you should stay in bed with me," I tell her.

"If this is your way of flirting, you're impossible to figure out."

"Uh, not that impossible, because…" It's not what I had planned, but I decide to go with it.

"Wait, is it working?"

"Who is the wolf?" she asks again.

"Just some guy," I say. "I'll tell you in the morning."

"Is he someone you're fucking?"

"No. Just lay down."

"I've fantasized about you telling me what to do," she says, "but right now you sound like an asshole."

"You can hold yourself up all night. But that seems uncomfortable."

"Okay, I'm leaving." She starts to shuffle backwards and almost falls off the bed.

"That's a bad idea," I say.

"So are you."

"I'm sorry," I tell her. "I won't touch you. Just get in bed."

She laughs in a way that sounds mean. "Oh my god." Then she starts walking away.

I say, "Please." When that doesn't work, I tackle her on to my mattress.

"Get the fuck off of me," says Sara. She's able to maneuver her arms out from under me and wrap her fingers around my neck. "I swear to god, I will kill you."

It's unintentional, but my cock starts growing. Within seconds, it's pushing at the seams of my hipster, Levi's jeans. The choking makes it better. More like a rock. Then it makes me pass out.

20.

THERE'S DARKNESS, TUNNEL VISION, AND then the image of my bedroom. Sara sits on the corner of my bed, watching. The zipper on my pants is down, and my cock is out. It's erect until I start moving.

"Hey," I say at some point.

Sara takes her time before speaking. "I'd rather not apologize again. So I'll just explain… I thought you were trying to rape me. 'Cause I felt your boner."

"I wasn't trying to rape you."

"I think I know that now."

"Why didn't you leave?" I ask her.

"Why didn't you want me to leave?"

"Because you shouldn't drive home drunk," I say.

"Drive home drunk or drive home? There's a difference."

"I don't know," I say while staring towards my flaccid penis.

"I was curious," she says.

"About my cock?"

Sara nods.

"We've already fucked," I remind her.

"Yeah, but in a movie. I never get to just look at it in a movie."

"It's there," I say. "You can look at it."

"I was hoping it would go down in your sleep. But it was just like…" She holds her forearm up and makes a fist.

"You want to look at it soft…"

"Is that weird?"

My head shakes from side to side. "I guess not."

Sara comes closer and lays her fingers on my foreskin. She pushes it up over the head of my penis. The rest of her is still. It's like she's zoning out on my cock.

It starts to get hard again, and she goes, "Wait. Keep it little."

"This is getting weird," I tell her.

"Just for a minute," she protests.

"If you keep touching my dick, it's gonna get hard."

"Sorry." She takes her hand away.

"It's not a bad thing. I'm just saying it's gonna happen."

"Right," she says. "I'll stop."

"Why?"

"Because you don't want to fuck me. And if your dick is hard, and you're awake, that's totally unacceptable."

"Then I'll fuck you," I say.

"Oh."

It's the last thing either of us says before morning and the last movement for at least a minute. There's inching over sheets, and hands on knees and thighs. We regress to the state of children in heat.

I'm stalling because I forget how sex happens in real life. Sara looks nervous. Once her pants are off, I remember what I'm supposed to do. It's a lot like work. Except I'm pressed to her skin, and holding her face down with my palm, and shaking. When I come, there's nothing to clean up. We let it drip, and stick, and hold us together.

21.

I watch Sara get dressed through the corner of my eye. Then I listen to her feet tiptoe across my apartment floor. There's a creak I recognize from my front door. And a loud thud.

I follow the sound to my kitchen foyer. Sara's on the floor, clutching a hole in her stomach. Her mouth makes noises like hissings and moans, but they're drowned by the gargle of blood she spits from the side of her lips.

Her eyes plead with me for help. All I can do is fall to my knees. Once I touch her, once my hands are wet, I'm more useless than she is. It's called panic, or shock. I've never learned how to deal with it. I bask in fear and silence until Sara is able to force something up from her throat. It sounds like, "Go…"

Suddenly, I'm reminded that I have feet, and that they work. That my friend is dying. Because I don't want to go outside, there's only one way left to reach the world beyond my apartment.

22.

"It's so good to see you," says Damien on Skype. "I thought that maybe you were mad about what I said the other day."

I bite my hand to keep from crying. Suddenly there's blood on my face.

"What is that?" he asks. "Are you okay?"

"I need you to call the police."

"But I'm in Canada," he points out.

"Please," I tell his digitized face. "Someone is going to die, and you are the only one who can save her."

"Can I ask you a question?"

I'm sobbing inside my head, but I think I manage to nod.

"Why don't you call them?"

"Because my phone…" If I say anything else, I'm not aware of it.

"Oh, okay," says Damien. His hands are fidgeting so fast it looks like they're convulsing. "What should I say is wrong?"

"Everything." I speak some numbers and the name of a street. "Make them come as soon as possible. Please."

"Yeah, okay." Damien just sits there.

"Why aren't you calling the police?" I ask him.

"Because I don't want to turn you in."

23.

SARA'S STILL LEAKING ON THE kitchen floor. Her chest moves up and down—slowly—so I know she's alive. There's a lot of blood.

I walk in a circle several times, then run back to my computer.

24.

WHEN I LOG ON TO the cam site, *TheWolf* is lurking in the free chat room.

"What the fuck do you want?" I ask him.

TheWolf: You're a slow learner.

TheWolf: But I have faith in you. I still want you to come over.

"She's going to die."
The Wolf: It takes a long time to die from a stomach wound.
"I'll do whatever you want," I say. "Just let me help her first."
The Wolf: Wear your red riding hood.
He types out the address once more.
The Wolf: It's not far.
The Wolf: You can walk here.

25.

THE RED, HOODED DRESS IS crumpled on the floor next to my bed. I must have pushed it off during one of my naps. Maybe when I fucked Sara. The fabric feels damp on my skin.

26.

SARA'S EYES ARE OPEN AND tracking my every move. She can see me wear the dress. I can only imagine what it means to her: a veil away from mourning, a colorblind funeral, or camp and drag at her expense.

"I'll be back with help," I whisper in her ear. I'm kneeling beside her and soaking up her insides with the fabric. The crimson patterns blend together in thick globs.

Sara whispers, "It hurts," while she squeezes my hand.

I kiss the back of her palm and grip it like a vice. Then I stumble away and leave her.

27.

THE OUTSIDE WORLD IS BRIGHT and haunting. There's a man on the sidewalk curb. His head is between his knees and he's rocking. I think to the rhythm of a tune he mumbles. It sounds like something that should be pretty. Inside his head, I'm sure it is.

When I pass by, he stares me down. Then he says, "Faggots," under his breath—like there's more than one of us.

I ignore the man and focus on something else: my hands. I'm gripping a small piece of paper that I don't remember bringing with me. It has a few digits and the name of a street scribbled on it. When I look up, a street sign with the same name pops into view. I've never noticed it before. I think because the street looks like an alley.

The choice to enter feels like death. I remember watching a war movie where a soldier runs in zig-zag patterns to dodge a bullet. I'm pretty sure I could do this. But *The Wolf* is an excellent marksman. I'm also wearing a dress that's longer than my legs. I'm already tripping over it. Maybe I could hold it while I run. If I wave the fabric around, the bullet might hit cloth instead of me.

The pigeon that's been grazing near my feet explodes. The feathers float around me like in a pillow fight. Except there's chunks of bird splattered on the pavement.

I run down the alley and search for numbers that look like what's on my piece of paper. They appear in faded rust and yellow.

I knock and the steel gives in. My hand pushes it further. I stare into a black hole.

28.

ONCE MY EYES ADJUST, I see a brick wall. There's nothing in the room but boxes and a metal staircase.

Because of the gun, I feel I better hurry. I clamber up the steps and face another door. This one's open, too.

It's brighter inside, but not by much. Staggered lamps glow with energy efficient bulbs. There's also a window cracked on the far end of the room—the one facing the street and my apartment. Sun spills across the floor in one long sliver.

Pictures line the walls. Some are painted—dogs, horses, fields, and streams. The others are photographs—a man and woman, various locales, a young boy and then the same one, but older.

The space is an open loft with several partitioned walls. There are no doors except for the one I walked through and what I assume leads to a bathroom (because of the sink outside it). The most frightening observation is that no one appears to be home. It's like I've followed the trail of a ghost.

"Hello?" I say with no response—well, almost. I guess it's just delayed.

There's a cough. Then shuffling and long, drawn out squeals—like metal on metal, or something tearing apart. A voice goes, "In here."

At this point, I've made my grave. There's nothing else to consider. Except for Sara's wound. If I die, then so will she. But if I step forward, there's a chance that things will change.

I stagger around the corner of a thin wall plastered with wedding photos and an equestrian beast carved in black wood. There's a bed on the other side. A young man lies atop it. He's on his back and still. There might be some tubes hooked up to his nostrils.

A voice comes from the direction of the man, but I don't see his lips move. "Come closer."

I do. My steps bring me to the foot of the bed.

Suddenly, the light above me goes dim. Another one shines directly in my eyes.

"What I want is less than you might expect," says the voice.

"Can you turn that away?" I ask, because I'm blinded.

"Please kneel down."

The fear brings me to my knees. Because I've likely been too cocky. And there's a gun behind the light. Or that's what I believe.

"Good," says the voice. "Now remove the pants." It adds, "Slowly."

The demand is vague, so I say, "My pants?"

"No."

All I can see is white light, but I lean forward to grip the young man's legs. There's no movement in his skin or bones. Not even a flinch. But he's wearing pajama bottoms, so they come off easy.

Next, the voice tells me, "Please find his cock and make it hard." It comes across like the word of God: directionless, omnipotent, and without material origin. It's clear now. The man on the bed is not the one telling me what to do.

I obey. Because the request is tame and I have to.

My hands fumble for limp meat. I pull at it, stroke, rub my other hand across the young man's scrotum.

"Use your mouth," says the voice.

I push my lips forward and slurp, suck, and inhale. The thing feels like an octopus flailing between my cheeks.

"Harder."

"I'm trying," I say between gasps.

The cock thickens, fills with blood, but never turns to stone. It's just bigger than it was before. I squeeze it at the base and pretend the skin is splitting.

"Your mouth…" The voice trails off and turns to heavy breath. Then it regains the form of words. "…is the most beautiful I've seen." There's more than lust. The voice carries adoration.

I keep moving my head up and down. It's enough to keep the meat from shrinking. In the back of my head, I'm thinking, "What's wrong?" Because he's still not moving. The body is like a warm corpse.

"Make it spray," says the voice. "I want you to taste it."

Maybe he wants to kill me. Maybe the young man has HIV, or even AIDS. Maybe I should stop. Because it's really fucking hard to suck limp dick.

"Faster. Come." And then, "Faster," again. The voice finds a tempo, urges me on like this is some sort of dance.

Then a spurt hits me in the back of the throat and I'm almost proud. It's like I've finished a race or marathon. But the prize is bigger than I expect. My cheeks expand with semen, and then I'm catching more on my lips, and up my nose. A lifetime of ejaculate washes over me.

I open my mouth and his seed gushes out. The cock drowns in it's own mess.

My gasps for air recede and I hear this: the voice—now a thunderous exhalation. Soon after, "Thank you." The gratitude is there but it's less eager. Or less turned on.

"Can I use the bathroom?" There's cum dripping down my eyelids.

"Clean yourself with the red riding hood," says the voice.

"Does that mean, 'No?'"

"You can do what you want."

"Wait," I say. "That's it? I can go?" It's not that I want more, but it feels like a trick. No one shoots a girl for a blow job.

The voice answers, "I'd like to thank you and pay you. But yes, you can leave." Not quite as an afterthought: "I'd appreciate your company if you decide to stay."

I smear the spunk on the red dress I'm wearing, but I still feel sticky. In a few minutes, it will dry and I'll just feel more like a whore.

Suddenly, the white light goes out and I'm enveloped in darkness. From blind, to blind, to blind, I'm beginning to forget what it's like to see color.

My other senses heighten as I listen the sound of staggering footsteps. They walk like a crescent from somewhere in front of me to right behind my back. Every few steps there's another loud squeal.

A steady hand falls on my shoulder and I forget how to run.

"I've tried what you've accomplished for the past two years," says the voice. It's whispering in my ear. "Sometimes I wouldn't find the courage to start. Sometimes I'd be in the middle of it and have to stop. Because I'd get sick and full of guilt. Or I'd remember his mother. So thank you."

The hand grips my shoulder, but now it doesn't hurt. It feels more like a massage.

"You're welcome." I'm trying to play along because it feels like a good idea. Better than anything else.

"I hope you understand," it continues. "It had to be you. Or someone like you. Most people don't understand sex as a ritual. Something with rules."

There are two hands on my shoulders now. Both are rubbing. Slowly, so I don't notice at first.

"You must think I'm mad because everyone has a rule— something that gets them off. A certain way to wank maybe." The voice coughs and the massage is jolted for a moment. "But someone like you… You understand how to play by other rules. Rules you didn't come up with. Rules you might not like. Rules even the one you're fucking doesn't care for. Am I right?"

I think about how to answer this, but end up saying, "I don't know."

"You're not really a hustler, are you?"

I shrug into his hands.

"A hustler would have done this. He would have sucked my son's cock." There's a pause there. Maybe to judge my reaction. I don't dare move. "He'd do anything I ask," continues the voice. "The difference is he'd think it was just for me. He wouldn't understand a purpose outside of the bedroom."

It continues, "I don't mean that literally. Anything that happens here is between us." It clarifies. "Between the three of us.

"Let me put it this way..." The hands fall off my shoulders and the phantom shuffles towards the bed. Then it falls, or sits, on the mattress. I still can't see. "I saw you in a film with a woman. Her name was...I believe...Carmella Deville. You remember this woman?"

I'm silent for a moment, then say, "I think so."

"She's much older than you, yes?"

There's no response to my nod. So I tell the darkness, "Yes."

"How old?"

"Older. I don't know."

"The Internet Adult Film Database says forty-five. Would you fuck her in real life?" asks the voice. "Would you fuck anyone twice your age for free?"

"Probably not," I answer.

"That's what I thought," says the voice. "I could see it in your eyes...when you had them open. They were closed for most of the video."

"I don't remember."

"Trust me. They were closed for most of the video. In your other videos, they're open. Most of the time they're open.

"Okay."

"So when you close them," it says, "I imagine there's a reason. Yes?" When I don't respond, it asks, "What is the reason?"

"Maybe I had to keep my dick hard."

"She doesn't make my dick hard either. But I found it interesting that she looked so bored. And bored from the beginning. I would understand that if halfway through the sex she looked at you and realized you were gone—lost in your own fantasy. That must be a turn-off for anyone. But she looked bored before the sex, during the sex, and after. She was just bored. It occurred to me that she might always look this way. It bothered me so much that I had to find out."

It's strange having a conversation with this thing, but my mind is on autopilot. Participation seems necessary. I can't keep from asking, "Why?"

"Because she's a beast—sagging, unkempt. No one would say she looks good for her age. And you..." The voice picks up again. "You're barely past your youth. Your cock is long, and straight, and smooth. You know how to use it."

"Um, thanks," I say.

"Why should she look bored? Most would be grateful."

"She probably gets booked with young guys all the time," I say. "It's a MILF thing."

"I found an interview with her," says the voice. "She said she hates it. She hates fucking young men. Because she knows they don't like her. She does it anyways.

"So she doesn't like fucking you. You don't like fucking her. Yet, you're fucking each other. The purpose is beyond the two of you." If I could see the figure behind the voice, it would be grinning. That's what it sounds like.

"It's a job," I tell this thing. So it will understand. So it will stop.

"Right. The purpose is money. The purpose behind the men who shoot it is also money. But the people who buy it…that purpose is not money. That's the purpose I'm getting at."

"It's simple," I say. "They want to get off."

"The men… How do they get off? They imagine themselves as you, yes?"

"Maybe," I answer.

"Even if they're gay, they probably want to see you have fun. I've done both—imagined myself fucking the girl. I've also imagined sucking your cock. Other cocks, too." It pauses, then adds, "I don't want to come off like I'm obsessed, but I am mostly aware of you."

The voice stops there, punctuated by another squeal. This time there's also a bang, or thud. Something heavy rolls around on the floor.

If not for the noise (and what comes after), it would strike me as odd. Because the point of the conversation is still not clear. I know something's happened. All I can hear is my breath.

The longer I'm left alone with my thoughts, the less I seem to have them. The part of me that speaks and listens, and determines what to do next—it stops working.

My legs cramp and sweat drips from my face. Panic returns. So does the fear of death.

Instinct had taken over to remove the pain. Like, if I had broken a leg in the forest and been forced to crawl back home. But not quite. The adrenaline made me numb, but it also allowed me to process information—to think. My body reduced itself to computational elements. It's all I needed to survive.

Now that the voice is gone, I'm back to something primal. That something needs to run.

There's a crash as I dash towards what I think is an exit. A knee-level object, hard and blunt, hits me and I'm on the floor. Then I'm up again in an instant, flinging myself between anything that's visible.

Around the corner of a wall, I see the sliver of light from the window. It's just enough to lead me to the door.

29.

THE SUN IS OUT AND I'm sprinting toward a Ralph's supermarket two blocks away. There's a pay phone there—I think. No, I can't think. My body must remember.

I grab the receiver. My fingers pound 9-1-1. But there's nothing. No dial tone, no buzzing. Not even the sounds of mechanical failure.

"That's not what I mean," says some guy behind me. And then, "Uh huh. Uh huh. Uh huh." He's talking into something small, thick, and plastic.

"Give me your fucking phone," I shout once I've tackled him to the concrete.

The man screams at me and bashes his hand against my face. Then he begins to crawl—only inches at a time.

We fight for the phone until he gives up and I break it.

People form a crowd and some run away. I yell, "Help me!" while crying. The water from my eyes tastes salty and a lot like come.

The cops show up and drag me towards a squad car. I'm cuffed and still screaming when I catch a glimpse of myself in the review mirror: red dress, blood, dried semen on the face, and tears.

30.

"My friend is at seven-fifty-five Miriam Place," I repeat to the cops. "And she's dying." This happens a lot before there's any reaction.

The pig who's not driving grabs a walkie-talkie-looking-thing and says, "Possible homicide at seven-fifty-five Miriam."

"That's all you had to say," I tell him. "She'll be alright?"

31.

They put me in a room with a small table a few chairs. I'm still cuffed.

"We found the girl," says a man without a uniform. "Want to tell us what happened?"

"Is she okay?" I ask.

He shrugs.

"There's another address you need to check out," I say. "I don't remember the numbers, but I can tell you where it is."

He sets his pen to a notepad. "I'm listening."

32.

THEY FOUND HIM ON THE bed next to his son—both of them close to death. He'd been dragging an oxygen tank around the loft and inhaling the stuff through a tube in his nose. I was told he might have cancer. Someone else said dementia, but I don't think you need oxygen for that.

There was a rifle in the apartment. And discharged rounds. The police confirmed that much.

I was basically off the hook.

"That's what happened?" said the guy without a uniform. This is when I finished my statement.

"Yeah."

"And you're willing to testify in a court of law?" He held tight to his disbelief.

"Should I have a lawyer or something?"

"You just told me everything," he said.

"I know, but…"

33.

THE WOMAN AT THE HOSPITAL desk believes I'm Sara's brother, so she lets me in to see her. I've brought flowers, but I'm not sure why. Sara won't open her eyes.

"Is she in a coma?" I ask a nurse.

"No," she answers. "She's probably asleep."

"Oh, okay."

"Please don't wake her," adds the nurse.

There's not much color in Sara's face, and she's hooked up to a bunch of tubes and wires. Other than that, she looks okay.

I lay the flowers on the stand beside her and sit down for a while.

"Would you like to be alone with her?" asks the nurse.

I sort of nod and the nurse leaves. Then I say, "Sorry," and try to touch my friend. Each time, I stop. She's beginning to look fragile, and I'm afraid she'll fall apart.

34.

THERE'S PAUSE IN THE CUSTOMER service rep's voice. "You have a warranty, but I'm not sure…it covers this?" He holds the phone up to his eye. We look at each other through the hole.

"It's okay," I say. "Just give me a new one."

"I can check with our manager, but…" He keeps stalling. "What happened to it?"

"It got shot."

"By a gun?" he asks.

"Um, yeah," I say.

"That's probably not under warranty," he says.

"I just need a new one."

"This phone, specifically?" he asks.

"A phone," I say. "Any kind of phone."

35.

I HAVE ABOUT TWELVE MESSAGES: some of them offers for work, at least one from an angry director (because I never showed up), and the last from Thad.

"Hey dude, did you get your amp fixed? I sent you some texts and stuff, but… Sorry, I'll text you again. Oh, I wrote a new synth part. Let me know if you like it." When I think the message is over, he adds, "It's in your email."

I text him: *Amp's not fixed. Been a rough few days.*

He replies a few minutes later: *Cool. We should rock out.*

I can't tell if he understands, but I leave it be. And everything else, too. I figure the world can manage a few days without me. In the meantime, I play video games and sleep.

36.

THE PHONE KEEPS RINGING. I answer it—finally.

"Christopher…or Danny… Which would you prefer me to use?"

"May I ask who's calling?" I slur into the mouthpiece. It's been a while since I've used my voice.

"Richard Walden, your lawyer. We'd planned to go over your testimony yesterday. Then I called to reschedule for today. And…"

I interrupt. "What do we need to go over?"

"Look, there are a few things I'm worried about… Christopher. For one, the reason you were at Mister Brown's residence. I read the police report. You admitted to…well… prostitution. That's not exactly legal. The defense is going to use it against you. They're going to want your testimony to appear less credible."

"I wasn't paid," I tell him. "So...like, does that help?"

"Maybe," he says. "I need to know these things. That's the kind of stuff we need to go over."

"How about tomorrow?"

"Do you know where my office is?" he asks.

"Yeah," I say. "I think so."

"Do you know how to get here?"

"Can you text me the address?"

"This is an office number."

"So can you text it to me?"

37.

There's a knock on the way out the door. Maybe I haven't opened it yet. When I do, there's a woman on the other side. She's middle-aged with brown hair, relatively attractive, and comes off as nervous.

"I'm looking for..." She trails off, then asks, "What's your name?"

"Um," I say. "You don't know who you're looking for?"

"I think you."

"Who are you?"

"I'm Gloria."

It doesn't sound like a real name, so I say, "That's a real name?" I might laugh a little bit.

She doesn't look offended. "I used to be married to... Legally, I'm still married to him. I haven't seen the man for two years, but I'm married to Ernest Brown." She's been staring at the floor, but her eyes shift to mine.

"Oh." I can't think of a better response.

"Do you think I could come in?" she asks.

"I don't know if that's a good idea," I tell her.

"I understand." She sways back and forth on my doorstep. "You saved my son's life. I just wanted you to know that."

A sickness washes over me and vomit surges towards the roof of my mouth. It takes everything I've got to keep from spewing.

"This is my number," she says, and hands me a card. "I'd like to talk some time. If you ever feel up to it."

My hand's over my mouth and I'm shaking. But I think she gets it. Gloria stuffs the card in my pocket.

In raised, black letters: *Gloria Brown, LPC.* And some other stuff I can't read because my eyes are blurring.

38.

"They're going for the insanity plea," says my lawyer. "Which, from what I've heard, may be relevant. But let's be honest, Christopher. No one wants to see this guy end up in a hospital. He killed your friend."

"Almost," I remind him.

The pen he's been tapping on his desk stops moving. "Maybe I misunderstood."

"Misunderstood what?"

"Look, something happened," he says. "I may have misunderstood."

"What did you hear happened?"

"I think you should call this number." He scrawls some digits on a piece of paper. "We can do this another time."

39.

Sara's funeral is ill-attended. There are a few industry people, and maybe some relatives—about ten of us, including me.

The priest asks, "Would anyone like to say a few words?" No one approaches, so he recites another passage from his book.

A woman stops me when it's over. "How did you know my daughter?"

"We were friends," I say.

"You look like someone she told me about. At least the way I imagined he'd look."

"What did she tell you?" I ask. My voice doesn't raise above a whisper.

"She didn't say it outright, but I got the feeling she loved him," says the mother.

"We were just friends," I say. "She probably meant someone else."

"You never know." And then, "Did you work with her?"

The question feels awkward so I ask, "What do you mean by 'work with?'"

She squints and says, "I don't know else to put it."

"We were both in the industry," I tell her.

"I hate to ask, but do you have any samples of her work? She'd never share it with me."

I'm caught off guard. "Do you think that's appropriate?"

"I don't understand. They're just illustrations," says the mother.

"Illustrations…"

"Well, whatever you call them." She looks hurt. "I mean, if it's a problem, don't worry about it. I'm just asking…as a mother."

The guilt-trip is worse because I can't give her the truth. But it's impossible to tell a grieving woman, "No." So I say, "I'll see what I can do," and start walking away.

"Wait," she calls after me. "How do I get a hold of you?"

40.

THAD'S FRIEND LENDS HIM AN amplifier head, and Thad lends it to me. It's enough for me to show up to band practice.

"Did you hear that Sara died?" he asks.

"Yeah."

"Is that why you've been so...?"

I thought playing music would be a good way to wrap my head around everything, or turn it off. But this isn't helping.

"Yeah."

"That's rough, man," says Thad. "I know you were close." He hits an arpeggiated note, then shouts, "Wait, were you dating?"

I pretend like I don't hear him and start to play a song. When I scream, there's no catharsis. It's just petty and muffled, and maybe only in my head.

41.

"STAY CALM," SAYS MY LAWYER. "Remember what we talked about." I think he means that I should try and keep from bawling. But he's never seen me that upset, so maybe he thinks that I'll get violent.

Anyway, I'm calm. At least I look that way when Ernest Brown walks across the court room.

Despite what he's capable of, the man looks like he's about to die.

A police officer helps the defendant to the stand and wheels an oxygen tank to his side. Then the judge says some stuff, and Ernest Brown puts his hand on a Bible.

"I do," creaks the man who shot my friend.

Brown's eyes go back and forth across the floor. They pause when they hit me.

"May I address someone in the room?" asks Brown.

The judge says, "Who?"

"I'm sorry I that I fainted before giving you the money," says the wheezing defendant.

"Mister Brown…" The judge's voice peaks upwards.

"I usually don't get excited enough to do that anymore. But our conversation was…"

"Mister Brown, you will stop whatever it is you're doing…" It's the judge again. "…if you plan to remain in my court."

My attorney leans towards me and whispers, "I don't think you need to be here. If you'd rather wait in the lobby…"

I nod and get out my chair. As I walk towards the exit, Brown sort of shouts, "It was worth it, Danny."

The look on his face is a mystery, because I don't want to turn and show him mine. Whether he's happy, sad, or pissed that I'm leaving, it's all a fucking blur in my head. Ernest Brown looks like a fog, and then transforms into one of those masks from a slasher film. After that, he's normal and old. I realize that all my visions of the man represent death. Or nothing. I guess they're both the same thing.

42.

My attorney, Richard Walden, meets me in the lobby. He doesn't wait for me to finish the game on my phone.

"I don't know if 'congratulations' is the right word, but it looks like this is over for you."

"What do you mean?" I ask.

"Brown switched his plea to guilty. You don't have to testify."

"What happens now?"

"He might have to undergo another psychiatric evaluation," says my attorney. "That's what his counsel's pushing for. But Brown just tried to fire them. My bet is that he's going to spend the rest of his life in prison."

"Oh," I say. "That sounds good."

43.

I'm HAVING PROBLEMS WITH MY erection at work. It might be the summer heat. Maybe I'm still upset about Sara.

I used to think death was romantic. Now, when I imagine having been in love with a dead girl, it makes me feel uncomfortable. I can't get over the sex part. The night we fucked in my bed, it felt good. Better than usual. I was getting used to standing still after climaxing on a girl's face. Waiting for photographs and baby wipes. Trying not to ruin a product. With Sara, I could just lay there.

I guess that's normal.

Sometime during the night, I felt like I could melt into her. In the morning, I found out what that would really mean.

The inside of her was just a mess. Maybe she had a soul or something. But I thought the need to know someone was more physical than that. Like, for a guy, sex is basically trying to get as far into another body as possible. Love is probably like that, plus something more.

I found some of what's inside Sara—the stuff people look for in a mate, partner, lover, or whatever. It's just that I don't believe you're ever supposed to get to it.

When she wasn't bleeding, I dragged my hands across Sara's skin and felt like each part of her was beautiful; like it wasn't possible to find something dull. Then I saw her on the floor. It wasn't anything special. Just scary.

I guess I could think about her blood like it was hair or shit, or anything else that leaves the body and dies. Except those things are dead by the time anyone sees them. What I saw was still alive. It was her fucking life force.

The fact that it was on my hands and clothes made it bad enough. I couldn't imagine melting into that soup, becoming part of it with her. It's probably a sign that I wasn't really in love. At least not with Sara.

I've been getting flashes when I'm about to stick my cock in a girl. They're hot, like the kind women complain about in menopause. I tell everyone around me to blame the sun. But my flashes are followed by the fear of what's inside these girls. If I get too far into them, I don't know what I'll find.

Instead of the feeling I'd normally get, I can't help but focus on my jaw. An eternal pressure sets in and I keep popping my ears to try and relieve it. Everything below my neck goes numb. The sensation of pulling at my crotch is almost outside of me.

The guy standing a couple feet away—the one with the camera—says, "No other director's going to give you this choice. Which one do you want to fuck?"

"Huh?"

"This one or this one?" He points to the girls like merchandise. "No one's gonna take it personally. Just tell me which bitch is going to make your cock hard?"

He's so severely misread the problem. It's hard to give an answer. "I don't care."

"Obviously you do, because..." His hand is a fist, and it's almost punching me in the penis. "Listen, you're about *this* close from never working here again."

"That's, um, not helping. So I guess I'm going home."

"What..." He's trying to stare me in the eyes but I won't let him. "...the fuck?"

44.

THERE'S NOT ENOUGH MONEY IN my bank account. I've saved nothing over the years, so a few weeks of hiding and a couple failed scenes is a financial nightmare. If I'm going to make it to my next set of bills, I need some low-pressure work.

"Oh yeah. I could start camming again." This is said inside my head, and in different words or thoughts.

Once I've logged in to Skype, Damien takes three hours to do the same thing. A couple minutes go by before he calls me for a video chat.

"I'm sorry," I tell him. "I've been gone for a while. Because, um, someone died."

"Promise not to get mad?" he asks.

"Okay."

"I've been looking for your name in the news."

"Why?"

"Last time we talked was kind of scary." Damien switches to his typical, needy demeanor. "Are you okay? I want to know what happened."

"Do you want to do a session?" I ask.

"Oh yeah, I know your time is valuable. Let me…" He stops mid-sentence and starts clicking on his mouse. "I'll let you know when it's sent." He means the money.

Honesty has never been my policy with Damien. But I don't feel bad telling him the truth if it means he'll feel sorry for me. Of course, the details can be left to my discretion.

"Did you get it?" he asks.

I check my PayPal account and say, "Yeah. Do you want me to do a show first, or…?"

"If it comes naturally. You know I love watching you do… that. But can we talk about stuff? I feel like we need to."

"We can do anything you want."

"I don't want to be selfish," he says. "You go first."

"What do you want me to talk about?"

"I'm worried about you, Danny. You look sad, and that makes me sad. I don't know how much of it has to do with me, but… Some of it does, right?"

"I don't think so," I say.

"Remember what I said about being in love with you? It was totally a joke. But you basically stopped talking to me. Then there was that thing with the blood, and you said someone died."

"Okay, I'm not mad at you if that's what you're worried about. But the blood on my hands was real. She was a friend of mine."

"Are you mad that I didn't call the police?" asks Damien.

"To be honest, I completely forgot about that."

"I'm sorry."

"At this point, I don't think it matters."

"That I'm sorry?"

"No," I assure him. "If you would have called the cops. I don't know. It probably wouldn't have made a difference."

"I'm sorry about your friend."

"Thanks, but you don't have to keep saying that."

"Sorry…I mean…" He looks around like he's hiding from his webcam. "I don't like giving advice to people who are better at stuff than I am. But do you want to hear some advice?" What he's said isn't that funny, but I act like it is. I try to compose myself before saying, "I would love to."

"When I was still in school, I knew someone who died. We weren't good friends, but I took math with him for three years and he always sat in front of me. When he stopped showing up to class, it was kind of weird. I felt like someone in my life had disappeared. They said he was dead…over the loudspeaker at school. It was very hard for me to keep from crying."

It's strange to see him get emotional, because I've never thought of Damien as a person. Now that I see he feels pain, I'm getting really fucked up about the way I usually treat him. But I can't really take guilt right now, so I'm just burning somewhere in my chest.

"There was some information in the principal's office about the family. It was so you could give donations and stuff for the funeral. Anyways, I called up Corey's, um… Corey was the boy's name. I called up Corey's mom and said that I was a friend. She cried on the phone with me for about an hour. Told me lots of stuff about him, too. That his favorite kind of sandwich was just tomato and onions on bread. And that she thought he was gay, and she'd never told him she was okay with it."

I recant on my own advice, and say, "I'm sorry you were so, um, effected by his, you know…death. Or that you had to listen to that."

"No," says Damien, smiling. "That's the thing. Talking to his mom helped. It was like a form of closure. Do you know what I mean?"

"I'm not sure I understand the advice."

"Maybe you should find a way to get closure," he tells me. "I don't know for sure, but I'd bet there's someone you can talk to. Obviously, I wish it was me."

This thing happens where I feel like giving Damien a hug, which is uncomfortable—if that can even explain it. I sort of massage my keyboard to make up for the impossibility of contact. Then I dismiss it. "Thanks, but…"

He waits for the rest of my sentence. It doesn't really happen, so he goes, "But what?"

"I don't know," I say. "I think I just need to jerk off."

Damien smiles. "Okay."

My cock comes out limp. I think it stays that way. There's some eternity of tugging, and I come.

45.

IT'S A FIRST. I'M TAKING the advice of a cam client and dialing the number on a card.

On the other line: "Doctor Brown's office, how can I help you?"

Me: "Uh…Gloria Brown?"

"Yes sir. Did you want to set up an appointment?"

"With Gloria Brown?"

"Yes sir, with Doctor Brown. Did you have a specific day in mind?"

"No."

"How about Thursday?"

46.

I DISCOVER SOMETHING ABOUT THE music I create with Thad: it's about nothing. Even the phrases shouted (tacked on) over the noise are gone because Mario quit—I think because he finds me so unreliable.

This realization is overwhelmingly comfortable in my current state of mind. The synthesizer, electronic drums, digitally distorted guitars, and pre-programmed bass; they can all be set to autopilot. I could just sample my own instrument and passively experience this thing washing over me.

Band practice is the perfect place to hide because Thad has all but taken over. "Did you hear the new track I sent you?" he asks. He plays it so I don't have to answer. "I thought it would be cool if you drone these notes over the beginning. Of course with, like, lots of reverb and delay and stuff."

"We're getting kind of good," I say. "Maybe we should play shows."

"Yeah, but where?"

"Oh," I whisper in the microphone Mario left on the carpet. "Good point."

We get through our set and I can feel everything. It's the appeal of the forest, ocean, and bustling city street. The sounds are familiar, but as if created by something else. It centers the mind, becomes like white noise. The world is peaceful until the mind wanders, body aches, and everything becomes a reminder of how alone I really am.

47.

MY ALARM GOES OFF. ITS purpose is amplified because it's the first one I've heard in over a month. Even though I get up to turn it off, it takes a minute to figure out what I actually set it for.

I eat breakfast first, check my email, and stare at familiar items in my apartment. The knock at my door is unnerving, but it gets my hopes up that someone wants to see me. That's why I open it a little too quickly.

The mailman doesn't sense my fear or excitement. He hands me a certified letter from my lawyer and a stack of other envelopes wrapped in a rubber band. I sift through them to pretend like I'm looking for something important.

"Thanks," I tell him without looking up. It's the same way he nods and talks under his breath. At the moment, we're a mirror. I imagine my life to have turned out like his.

When I'm back inside, I drop everything but the envelope still attached to my finger by a rubber band. It's from Ernest Brown. I feel like this should be impossible. Then I see the prison address.

48.

HER OFFICE IS LIKE ANY other. The waiting room is a place to sit. The desk, a place to house a secretary for eight or more hours a day.

"Hello," says the secretary. "Are you Christopher?"

"Yes."

"Perfect. Doctor Brown will be with you shortly. You'll need to fill these out." She slides me a short stack of papers. "I apologize if I already asked you on the phone, but do you have insurance?"

"How expensive is this?"

"It depends on your insurance."

I write my information on the papers until she says my name again. Then I'm escorted into a room with a couch and Gloria Brown.

"Hey." I wave.

The secretary leaves before Gloria can say anything. "I was going to call you. It seemed inappropriate to meet like this."

"Why didn't you?"

"This is an opportunity to talk, appropriate or not. If I'd discouraged you, you might have changed your mind completely."

"Look, I'm here. So I guess I want to be. But the whole doctor thing…"

She reads my mind. "I'm not charging you if that's what you're worried about."

"Okay. Yeah. Thanks. I mean, this was your idea anyway." I thought I'd have some control by standing over her. But I'm swaying so much that if she touched me, I'd fall.

"You can sit down," says Gloria. "I promise not to play therapist." It sounds like her version of a joke, but it doesn't help.

Still, I sit on the couch and sink. My posture inevitably fails me. "Um, you wanted to talk, right?"

"Right." She closes her eyes and exhales. It seems like preparation. Like she's got a lot to say. "'Thank you' is the first thing on my list, though I've told you that already. I just hope you understand how grateful I am. Whether intentional or not, you saved my son's life."

"I guess you're welcome," I say. "But I'm not really sure what happened. I mean, I know what happened to me. But I don't get it. I'm not sure you do, either."

"You may be right," says Gloria. "I'm foggy on the details. Maybe we can fill each other in? That's what I'm hoping."

"Sounds fair."

"You'd like me to go first?"

I nod, which means, "Yes."

"Where to start?" She laughs in a way that doesn't sound fun, or anything. "I'm usually on the other end of this… Well, I've been married to Ernest for, oh, twenty-five years now. We have a son together. His name's Joseph. He just turned eighteen.

"I separated from Ernest about a year and a half ago. It had been a long time coming. I'd been unhappy for years. He'd been…preoccupied with God knows what. I wasn't really interested in his life at that point. We'd stayed together because of Joseph. Because I thought it was good for him. Eventually, it wasn't good for anyone.

"Joseph was spending one week at my apartment, and one week at Ernest's. On and off. Mid-week at Ernest's, I received several phone calls late at night. I didn't answer at first. When I called back, neither did he. Ernest was prone to panic attacks, and I was fed up with dealing with them. I thought the phone calls were just his way of sucking me back into his bullshit.

"Ernest wouldn't answer his phone in the morning. I waited until after work to visit his apartment. No one was home. By the end of the week, the place was empty. I didn't see my son, or hear from Ernest, until you came along."

When I don't say anything, Gloria adds, "That's the short of it."

"Have you talked to him since?" I ask.

"Ernest? No. But my son lives with me now."

"What did he say happened?"

"Joseph?"

I nod.

"He doesn't remember. He's been in a coma for the past year. I'm sorry, I thought you knew."

"Yeah, I guess," I say. "I'd thought maybe he'd, like, wake up."

"He did," Gloria informs me. "That doesn't mean he knows anything. Even if he does, Joseph's been through a lot. The last thing he needs right now is an interrogation."

"So you'd rather pry the answers out of me?" I don't mean to sound like an asshole, but something in her voice puts me off.

Gloria reacts like nothing's wrong. Or, at least, she doesn't look offended. Under different circumstances, I'd think better of her. The fact that she's a shrink makes it less impressive. She's been trained to keep a straight face when people yell in front of her, or break down. I'm still a stranger. There's no emotional advantage to getting under her skin.

"You can leave if you want to," she says. "I'm not trying to pry. In fact, I don't think I've asked you a single question."

"Well, I'm not sure what I could tell you. I don't know what happened to your son. And your husband is…" I pause, but it's not to find the right word.

Gloria goes, "What? A fucking lunatic? You can say whatever you want. I'll probably agree with you."

"Look, it's hard to talk about."

"I understand," she says. "Or maybe I don't. Do you mind if I ask you some questions?"

"That might be easier," I say.

"All I know is what I've read in the newspapers and police report. Your relationship with Ernest was never really explained…other than that you were at his apartment to perform some sort of sexual service. Maybe that's all it was. If you don't mind, I'd like to know how you met him."

"Is that the question?"

"Okay," she rephrases, "How did you meet Ernest?"

"He was a cam client. You know when... Wait, it's okay to talk about this?"

She nods. "I'm not here to judge how you make money. I don't care."

"Okay. So you know when people jerk off on their web cams? He paid me to do that."

"And it progressed from there?"

"He wanted to meet in person, but I told him I didn't do that. Then he offered a lot of money. He suggested we meet in a public place first...a coffee shop. I thought he didn't show up, but I guess he just watched me until I left. I found out later that he followed me home."

"I know I'm not directly responsible," says Gloria, "but I'm sorry."

"That part wasn't that bad. I mean, it freaked me out. But all he did was give me some hooded dress."

"Excuse me?"

The therapist's shield kind of cracks, so I'm genuinely alarmed. "What?"

"I'm curious about the dress," she says.

"That sounds more than curious."

"It had a hood, yes? And..." She interrupts herself. "Sorry, it's nothing. Go on."

"Wait, that's not fair," I protest. "The dress was red and, I don't know...nice. Ernest kept calling it my red riding hood. You know something about it?"

"It was probably mine."

It seems stupid that the dress might be a clue, or some step on the way to closure. But it's the only thing someone else knows about my tragedy. The only thing that's not public.

"I'm not sure how to put it, but is it significant? Or... God, this sounds fucking weird, but it means something, right?"

Gloria moves around in her seat—readjusts herself, I guess. "Red Riding Hood is something he called me a long time ago. Not often, because I told him I didn't like it. Ernest only said it when I wore that dress...if it's the same one."

"So, like, he wanted me to be you?"

"I don't know what he wanted. That's part of what I'd like to figure out."

The answer is inconvenient. I jump ship to something mundane and nagging. "Wait, is Ernest gay? I never understand that shit."

"Given the evidence," she says, "I'd assume he lands somewhere central on the Kinsey Scale."

"What's that?"

"I mean that he's likely bisexual. It's the same for you, right?"

It takes less than a second to realize that she might be right. But I don't want to connect myself with Ernest. "I guess it's just weird that he wanted to get married."

"You're very young," she replies. "He grew up in a different time. I do, however, believe he loved me at one point."

"I never had sex with your husband," I blurt out to clear the air and make me feel less like a home-wrecker.

"It wouldn't bother me if you did," says Gloria.

"But I didn't. I don't even think he wanted to sleep with me."

"Why were you at his apartment? In your opinion?"

My mouth free-forms information. "He said a lot of stuff about rituals and the reasons people fuck and watch porn, and I don't know… He killed my friend so he could talk about some pretty stupid shit. It's not like this makes sense to me."

"Do you want to talk about your friend?" she asks.

"Not really," I say.

"Sometimes it's necessary to talk about. For your sake. It doesn't have to be with me."

"I'm not here so you can be my shrink," I tell her.

"I know. That's what I mean."

"Is there anything else you can tell me about the dress?"

"Not off the top of my head," says Gloria.

"Then I should probably go."

She almost stands up, but I'm walking out the door. My glimpse of her shows two balled fists and a bottom lip snug under her teeth.

49.

ERNEST'S LETTER IS ON MY desk—unopened—looking back at me as if it was alive. The decision to read it is over. I'm just trying to figure out when. My mood is already shit, and I'd rather not kill myself.

Also, there's a job tomorrow for a director I haven't fucked up for yet. Given my finances, it's a big deal I keep it that way.

I'm like, "I should probably sleep." But I'm not sure if it's harder to do while thinking about what could be in that envelope or actually knowing. An hour of tossing on the mattress suggests the latter.

50.

Dear Danny,

It was a great pleasure to meet you. I almost regret the circumstances as they will likely prevent us from meeting again. If you wish to write me back, I would be more than pleased. If not, I take no offense. I only offer my best to stir your mind in my direction.

First, I would like to implant the notion that I am not as crazy as you may have heard, but rather a victim to unfortunate events. If I may implant this notion, I would like to ask that you open your heart. Perhaps you'll find a place for me there. Not now, I'm sure, but one day.

In regards to you, there are some things I wish to have gone differently. I'd have liked to have paid your fee. I'd have liked to have stayed conscious during our encounter. Believe me, it's a point of great embarrassment to have nodded off so inconveniently, and without fully explaining myself.

Further, I wish your friend were still alive. I suppose it's an old man's pride to believe his shot is as good as twenty years ago. Picking that phone from your fingers gave me great confidence. I must have missed something with the girl. Or it could have been that her doctors were shit (a possibility not to be ruled out). If you hate me for her death, so be it. Just know that it was never part of the process.

"Then what was?" you may ask. It's a very good question. Because you have become an integral piece of this ritual, no matter how incomplete the thing now stands.

Since I am no longer able to gift you my material possessions, I would like to pass on the nature of my ritual, which is to answer the question you may have asked. It may strike you one day as important, and perhaps reframe the way you view your impact on thousands (millions?) of people. In order to give this answer, it is necessary to impart to you some history.

One piece of this history is the birth of my son, Joseph. Another is the day I came to terms with his homosexuality.

I found the first bit of evidence several years ago: a hundred-gigabyte collection of boy-on-boy porn on Joseph's laptop. The initial shock prevented me from looking away. After watching a dozen or so videos, I had to admit I liked them. I jerked myself in his room and climaxed several times.

Back then, it was nearly a miracle to get off once. You must imagine how thrilled I was to discover this new mental elixir. During the last video, it became clear how much more it really was.

People often debate on whether homosexuality is a genetic trait or a force of circumstance. I've rarely heard the argument applied to sexuality at large. It seems to me a great deal of traits lie dormant until something or someone brings them out. In the case of what makes us fuck, or desire to fuck, these traits are most complex. Rarely does one desire all cocks or all cunts. Rather, it is the specificity of a body, act, or context that defines a sexuality.

As I watched the men fuck on my son's laptop, I experienced the greatest state of ecstasy right before my final ejaculation. This occurred prior to my conscious revelation, and if I'm not mistaken, before the camera could have allowed it. I climaxed before viewing the boy's face, and yet my body understood the profound nature of our relationship. We were father and son.

It was a video of the poorest quality, and still the vision of his back, legs, and ass (mostly his ass) connected with something deep inside me. Whether Joseph's homosexuality was indeed genetically linked to my own was beside the point. My body knew it wanted his.

On a conscious level, it was quite distressing. To lust after one's own flesh and blood was both taboo and arguably disastrous. Yet, I lusted fully. My son's ass became the cause of every wet dream, and it formed the visions in my head when I fucked my wife.

The problem was that I couldn't have it. Anything was possible by force. But that was not my nature. Joseph was my son. While that was part of my attraction to him, I was still aware of my duty as a father: to protect, nurture, and so on.

That awareness further troubled me because Joseph was only fifteen and obviously a participant in illegal, amateur pornography. To do anything about it meant I had to admit I'd seen the video.

Of course, I said nothing.

I perused his pornographic collection often, and searched for more videos in which he might be involved. To this day, I've found only the one.

I had to accept the fact that I could never have Joseph in the way I truly wanted. So I settled for the next best thing. His porn collection tied me to him in a way I considered special. We inevitably jerked off to the same material. As his taste matured, so did mine.

Eventually Joseph became more organized with his collection. He would categorize the videos by sexual acts, or even actors. One day a folder appeared on Joseph's hard drive. It was highlighted in purple and the text read, "Favorites." Curious to know my son's preference, I opened the folder. There was only one video. You were the star.

He'd originally labeled your name as unknown. Then the folder—still highlighted—changed to "Danny Wylde." Pictures of you filtered in, but never more than one video. You were younger in it, and had a cock in your mouth.

I searched for you on the Internet and found many more videos. You were always paired with women. It occurred to me that the first video had nothing to do with your desire to fuck. Yet there you were, happy, and slurping at a cock.

On the brink of this discovery, I fell into a state of deep self-reflection. You and I were not so different. I fucked my wife and you sucked a cock. Both of us looked content. But we had moved on to something else. My wife could never truly have me again and those like my son could never have you.

This meditation shifted towards my relationship with Joseph. Evidence of our genetic makeup surfaced once again. In the same way I desired him, he appeared to desire you. We quelled our thirst with second-grade romps, but they were never truly enough. The objects of our affection, the contexts in which they mattered most, remained captured in single strands of data. Videos of less than thirty minutes held the keys to our sexual identities.

Thoughts of our condition flowed rapidly and I laid awake some nights scheming how I might one day achieve my body's purpose. One such night, my wife laid awake, too. She leaned over and tried to kiss me. When I didn't kiss back, she began to pack her bags.

Our separation was inevitable, and if you'd asked me then, perfectly timed. Unfortunately, I was unprepared to deal with Joseph on my own. The weeks he lived in my apartment were spent behind his locked, bedroom door. I gathered from our few bitter conversations that he blamed the separation on me.

My mood became distraught. How was it possible that I'd been given such a curse? First my lust for Joseph and then his utter hatred for me. Truth be told, I might have killed myself if Joseph hadn't beat me to it. As you well know, he was not successful. But my son did try.

The night of Joseph's suicide attempt, I was brooding by the television. A loud sound came from deep in my apartment and I first mistook it for a crackle in the speakers. Then I realized the speakers weren't on and that I was watching the screen in silence. Because I was thinking of Joseph, and the sound was most obnoxious, I got the urge to run to his door and tell the boy off.

At first I yelled something fierce, but there was no response. I knocked several times, again without response, at which point I nearly went to bed. But the resentment boiled inside me, and I knocked the fucking door down. Joseph was on the floor, noose around his neck, face blue, and motionless.

To relay what I felt is impossible. Just know that I have never been more consumed by grief. My body fell to the floor and I sobbed. Time stood still. What could have only been minutes felt like days. I held my son and wept.

When I felt his breath on my neck, I was in no state to react. At least not appropriately. The best thing would have been to call the hospital. I know that now. The worst would have been to fuck Joseph's ass.

I did the worst.

Understand, the act was reprehensible. Though removed from the world's sense of morality, it became the most free and ultimate expression of my true, innate desire.

I trust you to find some beauty in that—the state of fulfillment. It's something that cannot be imparted but by experience. It defies imitation.

The inside of Joseph's ass is not a word or an idea, or even a place. Not to me. It's a feeling of nirvana. Perfection. Wrapped around my cock, it filled my body with energy beyond matter. My pleasure transcended the natural world.

All I've ever experienced now sits rungs below this... I don't even know what to call it. Perhaps, a memory, for that is all I have of it. Now that I'm on the other side, nothing will ever come close. I know I've reached my zenith. My life is beyond purpose. It's because of this that I understand something most disturbing: I was never supposed to find nirvana.

That is why my most precious desire was placed inside my son. It should have been impossible to discover, so that life would continue its momentum. Without the joy of progress, the world stands still. Not only that. It begins to decay.

I didn't know it at first. Joseph remained in my care because I could not give up his treasure. My life's destruction seemed nothing

to do with it at first. At least, it appeared only as a byproduct;
a result of my selfish decisions. My cancer, Joseph's coma, the
loss of friends and career, the hiding, the suffering, and even my
incarceration: each was a cause of my violation. I had intervened
in the natural order of things, and ultimately set in motion my
demise.

If I had constructed this ritual of your involvement before
I'd fucked him, maybe things would have turned out different.
Perhaps I could have brought us all together. However, such things
remain a mystery.

All I can tell you is of my intent. Though even now, it must
wait. Prison allows for little luxury. I've filled this parchment as
much as I can and must wait until I find another. Until then, look
towards your light. But don't find it, Danny. Never find it.

Your friend and admirer,

Ernest Brown

51.

I CAN PROBABLY CONTACT THE post office or the police. One
of them should keep Ernest from writing me again. Or stop
whatever he writes from getting to my mailbox.

But if I think about it, the letter's done something. My eyes
have gotten blurry from reading it, or maybe just my brain. The
point is that Ernest's train of thought is so fucked that I haven't
been able to do anything with it. I've just started spacing out
and letting my body take over.

It's the perfect mindset for porn, which is why I'm almost
grateful. My line of work relies on severity. With tragedy, things

need to get too intense to process. Then my switch flips and everything works. My dick gets hard when it's supposed to, and the rest of the world fades out.

It feels like magic. Warmth, friction, pussy, whatever. I'm just stretching it. Getting inside. All that extra stuff isn't there: the person, set, crew, commodity, and my relationship to whoever it is I'm fucking.

Ernest flashes through my skull. The image I've constructed shows a father raping his son. Blood drains from my cock. Then his words come back, and the image blurs. I try the same thing with a picture of my father and it's worse. So I stay with Ernest, black out, and keep pounding flesh until I come.

52.

"Do you want to play a show around the first of the month?" Thad asks over Skype.

"Yeah, but how will anyone know who we are?"

"Oh, my friend's store is going out of business. It's a fundraiser thing."

"But how are we gonna raise any money if no one knows who we are?"

"It doesn't matter," says Thad. "There will be other bands."

"That makes sense."

"It's around the first of the month."

"You already said that," I tell him.

"So you wanna play the show, right?"

I nod and start writing something on Facebook about being in a band. "Where is it?"

"Um, I told you. At my friend's shop."

"I know, but like, what's the address?"

Thad shrugs. "Dude, I don't remember numbers."

"Okay, but you know what it's called, right? The shop?"

"Black Snow."

I type *Black Snow* into Facebook along with a tentative date: March 1st. Then I ask, "What do they sell?"

"Skateboards and stuff."

"Cool."

No one responds to my post. But a notification pops up on my profile. It's a friend request from Gloria Brown. I accept it because the picture on her page looks like it's from twenty years ago, which means she's kind of hot.

My body's back in *that* state, thanks in part to her husband. I instinctively start jerking. Then I remember how uncomfortable Gloria makes me. And that Thad is still watching me on Skype.

53.

THERE ARE MORE PEOPLE AT our concert than I would have thought. I guess it makes sense because it's not really *our* concert. Still, a bunch of kids watch me sway on stage (a wooden platform built to display shoes) and scream. No one's getting into it, but no one's leaving, either. I'd like to think they're trying to figure me out. As if I'm interesting enough to demand that kind of attention.

I notice more people looking at Thad than at me, so I start screaming something I hadn't really planned on. It doesn't make a difference.

After we're done, I hang around some skate decks and pretend to keep packing our gear. There's a boy with his eyes locked on me. I stop rewrapping the same piece of audio cable.

"Good set," says the boy. "I like the electronic stuff."

He sort of looks familiar, and I hope he is. Because I go, "Thanks," and then, "How have you been?"

All of a sudden, the boy looks really nervous. "Oh. I didn't think you'd recognize me."

Maybe we went to school together. Probably not. He looks younger: fresh, skinny, and emotionally complicated in the way only teenagers can pull off. Meaning, he's still attractive. It's strange. I don't usually think of boys like that.

I'm squinting like I should remember. Then I smile and confess. "I really don't."

"Why did you say…"

"I'm not sure. Maybe I thought you were someone else."

"Well, I don't know how to say this exactly. I've been trying to figure out a way to meet you. My mom said you'd be here."

It all comes together. I remember a piece of his face from the dark. The ghost of his semen fills my mouth like a sharp aftertaste.

"Your mom?" I say this in a way that should mean something else.

"Her name's Gloria," says the boy. "You know her."

"Right."

"If you're mad, it's not her fault. She actually doesn't want me to be here. But I insisted. Because I want to say, 'Thank you.'"

As of now, the whole family's expressed their gratitude. All for different reasons. I feel like I should be getting more out of this. Like, a new car or something.

"It's cool," I tell him. "No big deal."

He looks confused. "I'm Joseph Brown."

"Right."

"So… You saved my life. I think it is a big deal."

"I'm really glad you're alive, Joseph. That's cool."

"Can I take you out for coffee or something?"

"I don't drink coffee."

"Then how about dinner or…whatever you want."

"Listen man, I kind of have to pack up my gear."

Joseph backs off a little. "I didn't mean right now."

"Are you asking me on a date?"

"What? No. It's a gesture. Of my appreciation."

"Okay," I tell him. "Hit me up on Facebook, or Skype, or something."

"Yeah. For sure. What's your SN?"

I'm back to wrapping the same piece of audio cable. "It's just my name."

"But which one?" Joseph makes a face like he knows the wrong thing slipped out. "Never mind. I'll find you."

54.

"WE GOT SOME REALLY POSITIVE feedback," says Thad on Skype.

"Yeah, like what?"

"No one said anything to you?"

"Some people said stuff. I'm just asking what they said to you."

"Why are you getting all agitated? I'm just happy people like the band."

"I'm not agitated."

Thad's huffing and puffing. "You've been in a really shitty mood lately."

"Cool."

"Dude, you get laid for a living. You should be a happier person."

"I'll see you at practice," I say, and log off.

My web browser is still open and alerting me to Facebook notifications. There's a new friend request and message. Both are from Joseph Brown.

Dinner tomorrow night? Do you like Korean Barbeque? Hit me back.

55.

I've been working, but I wouldn't say enough. So it's more for the free meal that I accept Joseph's invitation. He's agreed to pay for everything. Probably with his mom's money. Plus, I like Korean food.

"You should try the pork belly. It's my favorite," says Joseph.

"Does Gloria know you're here?"

"She knows I'm at dinner."

"But not with me…"

"She knows that I'm an adult, and it's none of her business. I'm sure she'd approve of my motivations."

"Which are, I'm sure, completely philanthropic." I'm sarcastic in tone. Maybe not enough.

"Not exactly. I mean… Yes, I want you to get something out of this. But I think there's a lot to be gained here…for me. Psychologically speaking." He smiles. "Mother approved." He brings his fist down like a gavel.

"What do you want me to get out of this?"

"Um, a good meal and…" Joseph flips his hand around a few times. Fidgety kid. "A sense of self worth." I start cringing, so he goes, "That came out wrong."

"Really…"

"Look, I read the newspapers. They weren't exactly nice to you. I want you to know that you do a lot of good for people. You did a lot of good for me."

"Okay…" I start cutting a hand across my throat, a sign for him to shut up. "The meal's plenty. You can buy me a drink if you're still feeling guilty."

"Talking about this is off limits?"

"Say what you need to say. But I didn't do anything for you. No one needs to hear how 'good' I am."

"That's fine," he says. "Let's talk about something else."

"Perfect."

"How long have you been in a band?"

My eyes roll, but I answer. "A few months."

"Favorite color?"

Stuffing my mouth with meat, "I don't know what the point of this dinner is, but I'm sure my favorite color isn't part of it."

"What do you want to talk about?" asks Joseph.

"Would it bother you if I said, 'Nothing?'"

"No, but come on… Isn't there something you want to know about me? Ask me anything."

It's an invitation I wasn't quite expecting. Especially since I've been so comfortably self-involved. A couple things cross my mind—mostly having to do with the letter Ernest sent me. But they either seem inappropriate, or just too complicated to explain.

To throw the boy a bone, I say, "Yeah, okay. Tell me what you're gonna do with this good I've done for you."

"What do you mean?"

"You said I saved your life. What do you plan to do with it?"

"Like, what I want to be when I grow up?"

"Sure."

He's stalling and fidgeting again. I don't know him well enough to call it a sign.

"Honestly," says Joseph, "when I was younger, I wanted to be like you."

If his father's not a liar, I know what this means. I get the feeling it's not a big "if."

"Like me, how?" I try to force it out of him.

"The idea of getting paid for sex used to appeal to me." His eyes turn into droopy saucers, like a puppy's. I think to coax my approval. Because he shouldn't know this about me? That's what I'm guessing.

"I'm not a hustler," I tell him.

"I meant a porn star."

My eyes should be letting him know that his aren't working. At least not beyond their most utilitarian purpose. "Let me just say—before you go any further—if 'getting your dick sucked on camera' was the point of inviting me out, you should start feeling disappointed."

"It's not like that."

"And if it's more of a jerk-off crush, I'm also not interested."

"So I know who you are," says Joseph. "And yeah, I've probably jerked off to you. So have most people with an internet connection."

"You're reaching."

"The point is you're out there doing what you want to do, and you're successful."

"I admire your imagination…"

"You're so fucking modest," says Joseph, which makes me laugh in a quick snort that I hope retains some condescending quality. "Stop it," he adds.

"Anyways…Joseph… If I understand correctly, this no longer appeals to you. If you remember my first question, it had something to do with your future. Not what you used to think about."

"Wanting to be a porn star is still relevant. Because it has to do with you, and why I asked you here. I mean, other than the 'thank you' part you seem so weirded out by."

"I think you could benefit from a more direct approach with, I don't know, everything."

"My mom always told me I should find someone who's successful at what I want to do, and ask him for advice," says Joseph. "I've been in a coma for the past year, so I haven't had a lot of time to think about it."

"Okay."

"But I'm starting to think that everything happens for a reason. I mean, it's not just a fucked up coincidence that you're here, right? You're the guy my mom was talking about."

"Under the assumption that you're gay, my advice is to find someone—preferably a man with money and a camera—and let him fuck you. It might be more difficult if you were straight. But you're not. So don't think about it like rocket science. There's no trick to getting fucked when you're eighteen and look like… you."

"Do you own a camera?" asks Joseph.

There's silence. It becomes too much. "I think I need to make a phone call," I say, and get up to leave.

56.

I DIAL GLORIA'S OFFICE FROM the restaurant's parking lot. It's after hours, so there's one of those voicemails that asks, "If this is an emergency, please press 1. Otherwise leave a message." I press 1 and get forwarded to her cell.

"Hello?" Her voice is groggy and unprofessional.

"Hey, it's me. I'm eating dinner with your son."

"Excuse me?"

"I'm eating dinner with Joseph."

"Who is this?"

"Chris, Danny, whatever...."

"Oh. Is everything alright?"

"I thought you'd be more surprised. Now I'm getting the feeling you set him up. So, uh, what are you getting out of this? And really, just what the fuck?"

"I'm not getting anything out of 'this.' In fact, I think it's a bit inappropriate that you're going on dates with my son."

"This is not a fucking date. Believe me," I say, maybe too loud, into the cell.

"Am I to believe he dragged you out of your apartment? Listen, my son is in a very fragile emotional state. I suggest you remember that."

"Yes, and I've just gotten over everything, suddenly, and am living the most fulfilling kind of..."

"Why did you call me?" she snaps.

To put it into words takes longer than I expect. Longer than this phone call.

"Hello?" blasts into my ear.

"Your son is not my responsibility."

"So send him packing. He'll be all the better for it, I'm sure."

"Did you know Joseph wants to do porn?"

"Oh fuck you," says Gloria.

"He wants me to break him in."

"If you touch my son with your diseased-fucking-dick, I'll be sure you never use it again." She pauses for breath. "Are we clear!?!"

"He says it's your idea, so maybe you're the one who needs counseling, bitch!" I almost hang up. But first, "Oh, and tell your fucking husband to stop writing!"

57.

BACK INSIDE, JOSEPH IS ACTUALLY waiting for me, which either explains his naïveté or an understanding of human nature far more complex than mine.

"Alright," I tell him. "I'll do it."

"What?"

"If you come over right now, I'll fuck you. You're not getting paid though. And my camera sucks."

"Okay." Before he stands up, "This doesn't necessarily mean I want to do porn."

58.

MY WEBCAM IS STREAMING DIRECTLY to my hard drive: a room draped in shadows and dirty laundry. I'm not even sure that it's pointed at Joseph, or the cock I'm pushing in and out of his throat.

I grab him by the back of the head, and make sure the grip is firm. Then I shove him face down on my mattress, smother his head with a pillow, and beat the back of it with my fist. I'm worried about a possible concussion, so I switch to his ass for the punching bag.

Joseph makes all the right noises. When his mouth is no longer constricted by cloth and feather down, he tells me to fuck him harder. My hips pick up the pace, to which he goes, "Uh" and then "Faster!"

It's the opposite of stroking my ego. Because I thought I was giving him a ride—maybe something he couldn't handle. Now I'm pretty sure I conform to something less than his expectations. Just another real world top who can't keep up, or fuck deep enough to make it hurt.

I roll over without finishing.

Joseph looks confused, which is amusing since he's still panting like he's getting fucked. The novelty dies in about three seconds. He gets in my face, all worried-like, and goes, "What's wrong?"

Silence is all I can give him. Because I'm embarrassed, and it's my only way of flipping the dynamic. He'll either think I'm way too psychologically fucked up and start feeling sorry for me. Or he'll get fed up enough to leave. Either way, I'm on his mind. Whatever reason he comes up with is probably more interesting than what's actually going on. So I'm still a fantasy, and—I guess—in control.

"If you're not into boys, you can say so. I just hoped you were."

I can tell he's fishing because of the look on his face. And that he hasn't sunk his hook.

"Is it me? Or maybe you're nervous... Although you're a professional, so I guess that's not likely." Silence. "Can we at least play 'hot or cold?'"

My fetal position is turning inwards, becoming more cramped. If I'm projecting correctly, my body's a canvas of ambiguous pain.

"I tried this once before," says Joseph. "It was completely amateur. I guess this is amateur, so it wasn't lower quality or anything. Just sleazier. 'Cause of my age, and the guy who was shooting it, and it being illegal and stuff. Not that it bothered me.

"I think I was just nervous because it was different than the way I imagined sex. Every time I took his cock the way it felt good, the guy would stop and open me up. He was, like, fucking me sideways so the camera could see. And he was always leaning back. It was just his cock going in and out of me. I couldn't feel the rest of him.

"The guy with the camera kept saying that I was doing great. Then they'd both give me instructions on how to do it differently. Eventually, I gave up. I allowed them to position me and throw me around. My cock stopped working and I didn't really feel anything else.

"Afterward, they both fucked me in the bathroom and I came. And they came. And they told me I was a star, which was all lies, but it felt good at the time.

"I think it was important because, well… I've never told anyone this before. It's not like I trust you more than other people. I don't trust anyone. I just don't think you care. But it was my first time. When that guy fucked me on camera and when they both fucked me after, I think of it as one experience—my first time.

"I think the second part was necessary. If I'd just been fucked on camera, I'd probably hate sex. Maybe not hate it. I'd probably feel indifferent about it. Like, it's something that just happens.

"I guess I'm trying to say that I totally understand if this is weird for you because I'm not a girl. Or I'm just different than you imagined. But if you don't tell me to leave, I'm probably going to spend the night."

I don't respond in any way he can pick up on. So I guess he translates it to, "I don't care." He probably believes I feel this way about everything.

Joseph lays down and starts spooning me. I almost throw him off. But there's this involuntary reaction of something like warmth. My body can't reject him. Despite all the friction I've laid on other people, no one's ever held me like this. Not ever. It's the only explanation. Because Joseph is otherwise obnoxious and way too candid for my taste.

Still, I'm pulling him into me, wishing that our skin could melt into one piece. I don't even care when he gets hard and asks me, "Is it okay if I jerk off?" or when he comes on my ass, or cleans up the spunk with one of my shirts he swipes from the floor.

59.

COME MORNING, JOSEPH'S DISAPPEARED FROM my bed. But not my apartment. He actually brings me breakfast in bed.

"The eggs are a little off, but I think they taste okay," he says, handing me a plate.

I'm too sleepy to remember when I last purchased groceries, so I just go, "If you say so," and leave the food alone.

"You know, I feel comfortable here. It's pretty cool that you don't give a shit that your place is a mess."

It's one of those loaded compliments. I don't bother to thank him.

"My dad used to be in the navy. Making my bed, and stuff, was always a big deal."

"You were an army kid?" I ask, and recall an old friend from high school. He used to bitch about moving all the time. Different bases, or whatever.

"Not really," says Joseph. "He did all that before I was born. My dad's pretty old."

"I noticed." A sip of coffee. Mine? I don't usually drink the stuff. Not sure where else it could have come from.

"He was still into the lifestyle though. Shooting guns and being on edge all the time."

I think about Sara, and how she was probably just target practice for a piece-of-shit sailor. Then I sip some more coffee.

"I should probably get going," says Joseph. "My mom will be pissed if I'm not home before she goes to work."

"Fifty bucks says she'll be pissed anyways."

"Why do you say that?"

"I don't know. A hunch."

Joseph shrugs and crawls over me on the bed. He fights for a kiss and I don't resist. His lips stay long. Then they open and our mouths become wet. Before my cock is hard enough to do anything about it, he pulls away and disappears. I'm left throbbing and still.

60.

I JERK OFF, GO FOR a walk, and eat something that doesn't come from my fridge. Then I check the mail. There's another letter from Ernest.

61.

Dear Danny,

I've received no word from you, though I haven't allowed much time. In my imagination, you resent me. I just hope you read my words and think upon them. My only hope these days is that you come to understand me.

For such a possibility, I must impart more history. This time, on the subject of my former wife.

Things change. Though everything I've told you is true, it is also true that I once loved and desired a woman named Gloria Bennett. I even desired her some when she became my Missus Brown.

We met twenty-five years ago when I was stationed in Coronado. I was working my way towards towards Navy Special Forces. Gloria was a psychology student at the University of San Diego. Our romance began in a bar and continued in her dorm room. She was pale, thin, soft, and a bit naive, which I suppose met all the criteria I had for a woman.

Our sex was nothing to speak of. Nothing to interest someone of your experience. But I believe we both enjoyed it—my wife and I. It's sad I can't remember a single detail from the hundreds of acts we must have performed. It's old age, I'm sure. Also, the other side of me has taken over so fully. A woman—even Gloria, even memories of her—holds no importance to me sexually. She only serves as a reminder to something like innocence. That is a bit of what I've attempted to steal back.

Gloria and I had many pet names for each other. My favorite for her was the one she hated most. I had the opportunity to use it out loud for maybe a month. It was "Red Riding Hood." "My Little Red Riding Hood" is what I'd call her.

It originated on her birthday. I took her shopping and she couldn't decide on a thing. So I chose a dress. You already know what it looks like. It belongs to you now.

She looked beautiful in that red dress. I believe she wore it while I fucked her once. That's a detail. Perhaps I'm not so senile after all.

When I'd call her Red Riding Hood, she'd turn an awful mood. To compare her to a fairy tale was insulting, she'd say. It meant that I liked the idea of her more than the real thing. Maybe she was right.

In the version of the story I liked best, Red Riding Hood was the bravest of women. She gave herself to the wolf with the trust that the lumberjack would split open the beast and save her. She was a part of the weapon. If she didn't allow herself to be swallowed, the lumberjack would never come. The wolf would never die.

I explained this once to Gloria. She told me that I misunderstood the story. It was a patriarchal myth about virginity and purity, she said. I guess I've taken that to heart. As you know, I introduced myself as the wolf. Because I know I've threatened purity, and even destroyed it. My son may have been a sexual deviant, but I viewed him as innocent. He is no such thing anymore. Not even I can pretend it.

With my wife, I'd never broken her on purpose. Our disagreements came from a slow-burning disinterest. Go back far enough and she meant the world to me. Now I can't recall much about her other than I fucked her in a red dress. She's just a symbol. Like Zeus, or his daughter, Astraea—the celestial virgin. Or Red Riding Hood. She's no virgin, but in my mind, Gloria's the closest thing I've got.

I'll never see or speak to her again. That's why I needed you. Can you understand? Can you begin to realize your purpose in this world? You're a sexual medium, Danny. People live through you when they watch that little screen. You've learned to put up with it. I know this. You've confirmed it for me. You'll fuck whatever is put in front on you, and say any silly thing to get someone off.

Of course, you have a price. Everyone has a price. Not everyone has your ability. Most of us are too caught up in our own element. If I had your gift, I wouldn't be drowning in the fantasies that make up my existence. Why do you think so many people hate what you do? Hustlers, pornographers, anyone who turns more than a few tricks; the rest of us envy your casual relationship to sex. We've spent so much time thinking about how to stick our dick in something. It's unfair that you do it without a second thought.

You, Danny, are a special breed of this thing. You're not a simple hustler. I tried to tell you this once before, in person, before I fell ill. Your partner's pleasure is not paramount. Certainly, not your own. It need not be anyone in the room. I take for granted the cameraman seldom masturbates in front of you. It's the man from the future who counts. Or perhaps the woman. You give these people access to something they cannot have.

I needed you to be there with my son, as my wife, and in the present. The future is no good with something so personal. You brought us all back together—me, my son, and my wife. You also brought the lumberjack to me. If this were a perfect world, you would have disappeared completely. Of course, you would have been there. Though in my mind, you'd have ceased to exist.

It's still so hard to explain. I'm getting there, Danny. I just need more paper.

Your friend and admirer,

Ernest Brown

62.

On Skype, I ask Damien, "What do you think I do for a living?"

He answers, "Porn," then goes, "Is this a trick question?"

"No," I say. "But what about this? You know I do this for a living."

"You don't want to talk to me?"

"I want to talk to you because I need money."

"But what about when you…play with yourself?" Damien looks like he might cry. "You don't have fun? You don't want to do it?"

"Oh my god, shut up for a second." My face falls into my hands and bounces back. "I'm sorry. Don't cry. I like you. We're friends. Whatever."

His face brightens immediately. He's like a fucking dog.

"When I jerk off on cam, it's for you. Because we're friends." I kind of chuckle at this. "But you know I do it for money, right?"

"I like to know that you're enjoying it," says Damien.

"You don't think I'm doing it for someone else? Like someone in the future?"

He just stares at me.

"Please answer me," I say.

"I don't understand the question."

"There's no one else but us."

He looks lost and unsure of what to say. Then it comes to him. "You know that I always agree with you."

I log off.

63.

Hours go by. Nothing happens. At least to me.

Joseph arrives at my door in the late afternoon. He's surprised when I don't let him in.

"Don't you have somewhere else you should be?" I ask.

"Like where?"

"I don't know. School?"

"My mother says I should go back to school. She also says I don't need extra stress in my life."

"She's at work?" I ask.

"Always," answers Joseph. "If you want me to go away, just say so."

"I want you to go away."

"See," he argues, "I don't believe you."

I could slam the door in his face, but I ask, "Why's that?" which I guess gives him clout.

"You were checking me out."

"At the skate shop," I remind him. As far as I'm concerned, it was years ago.

"No," he counters. "When you opened the door. Words are the least important way we communicate. I read that somewhere. So you said some stuff. But I've been getting all kinds of signals."

"You're saying you can read my mind?"

"I'm telling you that I read body language. And I'm good at it. When you're under eighteen and guys want to fuck you, it's really hard for them to verbalize it. They're afraid of getting in trouble. If I make an effort to notice, it's easier for them to make it happen."

"Uh huh."

Joseph exhales. His breath says, "It's obvious that…" His voice, "I've had a lot of practice."

"I'm still talking to you, so maybe you're right about words. But you're misinterpreting everything else. If I want to fuck you, it's because I'm broke and no longer trust my erection. You're the closest thing I've got to practice. If I can come from fucking you, I can probably deal with anything."

"That's really mean," he says. "It's a good thing I don't trust words."

Joseph pushes me aside and wanders through my kitchen, looking for food. "You should get your fridge fixed." He fingers the bullet hole. "It's letting all the cold air out."

"There's nothing in my fridge to go bad."

"For the future," he insists, "you might want to get it fixed."

"Most of the girls I fuck in the ass—on camera—starve themselves before the scene. It's so they won't shit on me. If you want me to get excited about fucking you, maybe take that into consideration."

"I know I've been out of the game for a while. But take my word for it. I'm more than a novice. We went out to dinner and I didn't shit on you."

The kid's got a point, so I say, "True." Then, because he's still in my kitchen and looking for food, I go, "Well, there's nothing here anyways. Not in my fridge. Not in the cupboards. Maybe we should just get to the point."

"Wow. Yeah, that sounds like you just need... What did you call it? Practice?"

"I've got a lot of stuff to do," I lie.

Joseph gives me a high-eyebrow look that's basically the gayest way of calling me on my shit. Then he brushes past me towards the bedroom.

I wander in behind him and find the boy on my bed, on his hands and knees, face to the wall, and ass pointed up. His back is arched and everything.

"If a girl wanted to be a bitch," he says, "she'd skip the blowjob and just sit here, right? Waiting for you to get hard? You can practice, Danny. I promise I won't look."

I unzip and start stroking. Not sure if it's habit, or because I have something to prove. But it's working.

"Oh my god, what's taking so long?" Joseph heckles. It's only been a minute. "Think of me like some porno bitch." The boy spits on his hand and starts rubbing his hole. The sphincter pulses and swallows his fingers.

Three steps towards him and I'm mounted. Joseph's hands hit the mattress, his face rocks forward, and he falls flat under my weight. I look at my crotch and the space moving between his ass. Pieces of his skin stretch out like boy labia hugging my shaft. My cock fattens as I dig into him.

It's subtle, but his hole smells different than a girl's. Muskier or dirtier maybe. Once I give myself over to it, it's better in the way a new song feels the first time you hear it. I wonder if it'll be the same in a month. I can't plan far enough ahead to know if I'll discover it as more or less than a one-hit-wonder. Or for me, one-and-a-half listens.

To get the most of him now, I dig my thumbs into his ass along with a few fingers. With my cock in the middle, the sensation is perfect: tight and full. "I wish I could hit the back of you. Pound the spot where your guts stop and there's just… I don't know. I want to fuck your stomach. "

When I say things like this—sex things—they're nearly inaudible. It works when I'm biting someone's ear because the "fuck"s and "oh god"s make it to the right place. Pounding the boy from behind, I don't expect him to hear anything. It's almost weird that he does.

"If your cock can't reach it, come inside me," he moans. "I want as much of you as I can get."

I should probably ask if he's serious. Right now, my brain doesn't care. There's no one watching and no rules for me to break. Fuck communication. Our relationship isn't even based on spontaneity. It is spontaneity. If he's upset about it later (spraying semen up his ass), I always have the upper hand. Like, "You think I'm irresponsible? Your dad killed my friend."

Joseph doesn't seem to care. I release inside of him and he just keeps humping me. When I'm spent, he's still jerking. My cock softens as he shoots all over my comforter and falls into his own mess.

We're stuck together again, damp on my own bed. This time I'm riding my own endorphin high. When Joseph rearranges himself, the arms wrapped around me aren't so strange. I have to keep relearning. This is what I'm supposed to do when no one's there to say, "We're done filming," or tell me, "There's a shower in the next room." It might be an innate response to hold on to the person I've fucked. Evolution or whatever. I know I can't impregnate him, but my body doesn't. It wants to make sure I'm passing something along.

Maybe that's the trick to love, and why people with kids start to hate each other. After enough DNA's pumped into the same person, instinct takes over to say it's been enough. The breeding ground's been tapped out.

Joseph's ass is still fresh for making children. That's why it feels good to hold him and inhale the sweat from his skin. I won't get up and waste even one drop that might find it's way to life.

Okay, but instinct's fucking stupid now. Evolution breeds poverty and fat people. Aside from white trash and third-world peasants, everyone else is too scared to lose their consumer freedom, or else they're like Joseph—not scared of or interested in the most basic way to make a kid.

"What are you thinking about?" asks Joseph. "You look like you're in love with me."

My heart sputters, which is not what I want. I can't get mean or sarcastic. I'm just rubbing his nose with mine, and kissing him. Instinct. Evolution.

"Silence means 'yes,'" he says. "Especially when you're doing that."

"Shut up," I tell him, totally cute and whispered.

He bites his lip and smiles. I lick his chest.

"After this," I say, "I want to go for a run."

"Why?"

"I feel like you're giving me energy. And I haven't really exercised in a while. You can come with me if you want."

"No, I'll stay here," says Joseph. "Or, um… Do you have an extra key?"

"Somewhere."

"If you find it, I can get us something to eat."

64.

"This is the epitome of health," I tell myself. Pounding pavement after I've already been sweating. Everything's on fire in a good way.

Even though I'm broke, there's an eighteen-year-old waiting for me at home. Strange he's a boy, though. Not sure I've wrapped my head around it. Unless heterosexuality's an indoctrinated myth, which I would totally believe. I mean, look at prisons. Once a guy's locked up, it doesn't matter. Either he's a bitch, or someone else is his.

Here I am—not in jail—doing this thing with Joseph. Kind of getting hard while running. Meaning I'm still thinking about fucking him. Still freaked out that he comes from terrible people. At least one terrible person. And a bitch. Everyone hates their parents though. What's the difference if I hate his, too?

Too much thought put into this already. It would be cool if he spent the night again. But I'll probably kick him out tomorrow. I can't afford for him to stay with me. Unless his mom pays for everything. That would be cool. She owes me money anyways. Or her husband does. Since they're still legally married, they have the same debts and stuff. Like, credit scores and paying for hustlers like me.

After running a bit more, I realize how out of shape I am. I have to turn around to make sure I won't collapse before I get home. That's not entirely true. More like I want to save my energy for later. Fucking Joseph (again) seems inevitable.

65.

THERE ARE VEGGIE BURGERS ON the table when I get home. Joseph's taking bites from one of them.

"Why not real meat?"

"I read on Facebook that animal flesh is acidic," he says. "It causes cancer."

"We ate meat the other night."

"I read it yesterday. And I've been in a coma, so give me a break. There's a lot to catch up on."

There were vegetarians before his coma. Since the beginning of humans I'm pretty sure. Whatever. I tell him, "Thanks for the burger," and put it in my mouth. It's nothing like an animal, but still pretty good.

"Do you think I could fuck you?" asks Joseph. "I mean, I'm not sure I'm a top. I've never really tried it."

"I've tried bottoming," I say. "It's not really my thing."

"Oh. Still, would you let me fuck you?"

"It wouldn't be my preference."

"That's not a 'no.'"

I can't pinpoint the source of my ambiguity. Maybe it's the threat of rejection. He seems so into me, and not in a way I can't stand. I'm almost sure that whatever I say won't change that. "No" is such a weird word, though. Especially when it comes to sex. It sounds kind of prudish.

"Theoretically, if you did fuck my ass, you wouldn't be allowed to come. Not inside me anyways."

"Why not?" He sounds more curious than upset.

"I don't know. It seems really personal."

Joseph rolls his eyes. Probably because I squirted in him without second thought. "If you think I have something, we could find out. But if I have something, so do you. Right? Do you think..."

My cell phone buzzes. I answer the call instead of Joseph. It's a porn director who wants to book me. Obviously, I say, "Yes."

When I hang up, my attention's back to Joseph. "I have to work in a couple days, which means I have to get tested. For STDs and stuff."

"What's 'stuff?'"

"Just STDs. You can come along to see if you have anything. I'm not paying for your test though."

"How much is it?" he asks.

"One hundred twenty dollars."

"I'll ask my mom for money."

"Don't do that," I blurt out.

"Why? It's not like I'm going to tell her what it's for."

"Then totally do that."

"What if I just fuck your face tonight? You can still do whatever you want to me."

"Yeah, sure," I say, trying to sound indifferent. Really, it's the most interested I've been in sucking cock. Probably ever. Funny I didn't feel the same way the first time it was presented as an option. He still doesn't know that I've tasted him. Maybe I should tell him. Maybe later.

"Let's take a shower first."

"I was going to anyways." Of course. Because I'm still a top. I don't need suggestions about how to smell or be clean for an eighteen-year-old boy.

66.

How to do it when it's not for money or at the end of a gun? The feeling's not that different. Same texture. Sort-of-same smell. The soap helps.

Joseph's watched a lot of porn, so I'm gagging and using my throat as a shield. Taking it like a champ. I pull his cock out and hold it. "If you keep doing that, I'm gonna throw up."

"That's hot." He's back to jackhammering my esophagus.

The surge comes up and layers his cock with vegetable mush. Some of it hits my bed. My sheets are turning to polka dots of body fluid, and now this.

"You sure about your ass?" he asks. When my response is just a gargle, he blasts me in the throat and relaxes on the mattress. "You can do whatever..." His eyes are closed, so he's just offering one of those sleep creep scenarios.

I roll the cum around in my mouth, and try to remember whether I like it in general. Try to decide whether I like his more or less. Once the texture's been established, I guess there's something sweet in the aftertaste. Still, it's like swallowing oysters or snot. I guess I'm into one of those.

"You're gonna be there for a while, right?" I say to Joseph.

"Yeah."

"Cool. You look hot... But I think I need to cam a little bit tonight. If you stay the night with me a lot, just know that's something I need to do."

Joseph's eyes are still closed. "Sure."

67.

I POSITION THE LAPTOP so the webcam won't pick up Joseph. Then I log in to the cam site. A few guys filter through my chat room and ask how quick I can come. My response is always, "I don't know," because I need digital cash, and two minutes means less than a minimum-wage pop shot.

MrFluffer: Y do u charge so much?

MrFluffer: Other boys charge half. Makes more sense.

"Do you know who I am?" That broke, middle-of-the-road porn dude. The star of a thousand pirated tube videos.

MrFluffer: Think I saw u on Reddit.

MrFluffer logs off. Fucking Walmart, bargain-bin lurker. I'd believe it if someone told me corporations figured out how to exploit sweatshop cam labor. Slave masturbation. Boys locked in cold, dark rooms, forced to stroke their cocks for twelve hours a day.

To beat the game, I hop on Skype. I'd rather deal with Damien than haggle anonymous, black text. Except he's not here, so my "friends" think I'm being social.

Thad: Feeling better?

Me: Better than what?

Thad: Nevermind… How interested are you in recording an EP together? I have a friend who will only charge $400/day.

Me: That seems expensive.

Thad: His normal rate's $600.

Me: Oh. How many days?

Thad: I don't know. Depends on how many songs.

Me: Like the idea. Might have to wait on the money.

Thad: Will set something up. Can always move the date.

Thad: See you tomorrow.

I look at the bed. Joseph's still asleep, which is good. Because Damien just logged on.

He immediately goes cam-to-cam and looks like a beaming, pixellated mess. Like I've never been a dick to him in his entire life.

"Can I tell you what happened today?" he asks. The swiveling in his chair is already making me nauseous. Not because of motion sickness. Because it looks fucking embarrassing.

"Sure," I say. "Um, are we doing a session?"

"Let me tell you first. I'll be really quick."

"Okay, so tell me." I rub my eyes and look somewhere else, instantly distracted.

But Damien's voice is hard to miss. "Who's that?"

I look over my shoulder. Joseph's standing up and stretching. He's still naked.

From Damien again. "Who is that?"

"No one," I say.

"Why is he in your house?"

"Obviously, he's a friend."

Another question from Damien. "Why is he naked?"

"Jesus... Do you want a session or not?"

The pixellated mess is close to tears and pushing his face past the point of webcam focus. He's also getting demanding. "Danny...tell me the truth. Please!? This is more important than anything else. I know you don't love me, but I KNOW we have *something*. But...but...if we don't have something... I'm not willing to live with that. Do you understand?"

I'm sort-of waving my hand towards Joseph, trying to get him to leave, and nodding in agreement to...I'm not entirely sure what.

"Do you understand?" The tinny computer speakers' sounds are blowing out. I think because Damien's shouting.

"Uh, yeah. Totally."

"Is he your boyfriend?"

Joseph puts his weight on my back and leans over my shoulder. He also starts laughing.

"Dude, tell him we're friends," I say.

"We're friends," Joseph tells the computer screen. "'cause friends can be boys and boyfriends fuck."

Damien's collapsing. His face is getting snotty. It's a million times more embarrassing than the swiveling. If it weren't for Joseph's contagious smile, I might actually be able to empathize. Like, picture Damien as one of those dying kids on TV. Instead, I'm trying not to laugh at him.

The wailing crescendos. Damien says, "I hate you," and logs off Skype.

Then I snap. "What the fuck is your problem?"

Joseph looks at me like I'm out of line. "How much does that guy pay you anyways?"

"It adds up."

"I don't believe that person has a job." Joseph gets close to the monitor as if Damien's image will suddenly reappear. "So it can't be much."

My fist punches him somewhere between playful and hard. It's mostly a cue for him to knock it off. The boy backs away and I say, "He pays me."

Rubbing his bruising arm, "With what?"

"I don't know. Credit cards."

"That's fucked up," says Joseph. "Do you know much of an issue consumer debt is in this country?"

"What?" Like I don't understand him.

"I read it on Facebook…"

"Fuck Facebook and fuck you!" I slam Joseph against my front door. "What the fuck is wrong with you? Your family inbred or something? You all have no fucking clue how anything works and you don't give a shit about anybody. Whatever the fuck is going on in your head, you've got to put it out there, huh?"

Joseph tries to slither out between my hands and the door. When he does, I figure he'll just run away. But the boy clocks me in the face. My nose cracks and feels wet. I can taste blood in my mouth.

"What the fuck is wrong with me?" Joseph towers above me as I clutch my nose and roll around on the floor. "You hate talking to that guy. You should see yourself… Listen to yourself. It's fucking pathetic. He thinks you're his boyfriend…"

I spit words and blood, and something in my defense. "It's called a job. If you had one, you might figure out why everyone hates them."

"Man, I thought being a porn star would be cool. You live in a shitty apartment, you're broke, and you hate fucking everything. You're what? Twenty-five, twenty-six? Your entire reality is being a bitter piece-of-shit."

"You don't have it too good either, kid. You lost a year of your life 'cause your dad fucking raped you."

To this, I receive a kick in the ribs. "Okay! Okay, stop! I'm sorry."

"My dad didn't rape me." Joseph paces my kitchen and kind of mumbles to himself.

Because I need to clean myself up or get to a doctor, and at least one of them soon, I ask, "Are you going to leave?"

Joseph stops and stares down at me. It's like he's broken from a trance. "You need help and you don't have anyone else."

"Oh my god, go!" I try to swing at him, but he dodges. "You think I suck, that I'm an asshole. I don't even know why you're here."

"Why did you say that about my dad?"

Good question, because this seems like the worst time to answer. I groan, and mutter, "Can I get an icepack first?"

Joseph nods, so I crawl towards the fridge. Luckily, the freezer doesn't have a hole in it. Everything's still cold. I grab a packet of frozen vegetables and hold it to my face.

"So?"

There's a crusted, dirty steak knife on the counter, which I grab to say, "I'll show you. But you have to promise not to freak out."

"What are you going to do with that?" He smirks.

"Just…fucking… Don't hit me." I shake my fist and add. "And say you'll leave."

"When?"

"Are you serious? Tonight."

Joseph's not phased. "If you want me to, I'll say it. But you shouldn't believe me."

"What?" I thrust the knife, but not exactly towards him.

"There's a lot people miss because of…not sure how to say this. It's intangible. I go off feelings, Danny…"

"That's not even my name."

"Sorry. But it's one of your names. So Chris…I go off intuition. Meaning, most of my life has pointed me here. Knowing that, you think I'm going to run back to my mom?"

"You don't have a choice. It's my house."

"It's not a house," he says, like it somehow changes the point.

"Okay, so what? What does that mean? We live together now and I don't have a say in it?"

"Stop avoiding the subject," he says. "You said something really fucked up and I want to know why."

There's a question as to why I do or don't do things, and why I'm conceding to someone who just broke my nose. I don't have an answer, except maybe that right now I'm worried about my face and a kitchen stalemate won't fix it. Also, giving people what they want is what I'm best at. Even better when I don't want to.

"Fine." I put the knife down and move past him. Slowly. Once in the bedroom, I shuffle through some drawers and gather the letters from Ernest.

Joseph lingers in the doorway.

"I guess have a look," I say, and toss the papers on my bed.

He approaches and fingers the notes. That's when I slip by him and make my way to the bathroom.

68.

THE FIRST THING I IMAGINE is killing Joseph and flushing his body down the toilet. But I'm not the killing type, and the toilet thing sounds impossible once I think it through. My mind is just trying to imagine a world less complicated. One where the boy doesn't exist. Murder is the boring way out, a concession to television clichés. On the other hand, it could land me free food and a place to live behind bars. I could even find Ernest and slice him up too. What would they do? There'd be no place worse to send me and I'd still eat for free.

I stare at myself in the mirror and imagine other things: the doctor's bill, the money I'd need to pay for it, and the jobs I won't get looking like this. Fear sets in because I don't have it in me. Not to kill or even apply for a real job. Maybe enough problems to get locked up in a place less shitty than prison.

Maybe a psych hospital. Joseph's mom could probably make it happen if I pleaded with her or pissed her off enough.

There's enough motivation in my hands to wet a wash cloth and wipe the blood from my face. And enough self-pity to let my eyes flow.

69.

"We have to write him back," says Joseph, still sitting on my bed.

"What? I need a doctor."

"Is it broken?" he asks, suddenly concerned.

"Are you serious?"

"I'll take you first thing in the morning. No doctor's office is open right now…unless you want to go to the hospital."

"You're not leaving?" Why I say it as a question is beyond me.

Joseph goes, "Come here," and even stands to bring me over to my bed. He's being sweet. Brushing my hair as if it was long enough to sweep from my eyes.

When I'm more relaxed and getting massaged by his fingers, he asks, "Why didn't you tell me?"

"I don't know." I'm not so sure on the specifics, so I continue. "Tell you what?"

"That my dad was writing you. Anything about it."

Joseph's hands stop feeling good. They're like insects on my skin. "First, you didn't ask. And how long have I known you? We're fucking because… I don't know why. I'm not really sure—at this point—our relationship is consensual."

"A non-consensual top? I don't think that exists," says Joseph. "Whatever you feel about our 'relationship,' you owe me at least one answer." I wait for him to spell it out. Within moments, he surrenders. "What did you do to me when I was in a coma?"

I forgot he'd see that detail. My silence continues because I don't know what to say.

The act wasn't cruel or unusual. Not in and of itself. But I'm the one complaining about non-consensuality. I guess the blowjob wasn't fun if he didn't want it or can't remember.

"Did you fuck me?" he asks.

A quick, "No."

"Then what?"

"It wasn't like I wanted to."

"Did you hurt me?"

"No, nothing like that," I say. "I just sucked you off."

Joseph almost smiles. "Really?"

"It's fucking weird telling you this, but yeah."

"My dad invited you over to suck my dick?" he asks, confused. Maybe amused.

"He didn't 'invite' me over. He fucking shot at me. He shot at me and murdered my friend. I was trying to save her life."

"I don't understand," says Joseph.

"Neither do I. I guess that's my reason for not saying anything."

"Don't you think we should get back at him?"

"He's in prison...for life."

"I'm not mad that you sucked my dick," says Joseph. He tries to touch me again. I flinch. "But I think we should write him back. Get into his head before we kill him."

I stare at him for what seems like a couple minutes. Then I stare at the wall.

"What do you think?" asks Joseph.

"We should probably go to sleep. I think we've both had a long day."

When I crawl in to bed, I'm alone. Though before I fall asleep, he's there beside me. His cock presses against my ass, growing.

70.

WE STOP BY JOSEPH'S MOM'S house on the way to the clinic so that he can steal some of her money. He wants to get tested for STDs and insists on paying for a doctor to check out my nose. The doctor part is the main reason he's still around. At least, that's what I tell myself.

He says something different. "I can help with a lot of things. Give me some time and I'll come up with rent money too."

I don't really answer him. But he doesn't sound like he needs an answer. Joseph's talk of the future—the realm of the theoretical—is all I hear until we get to the doctor. A lot of it sounds like we're getting married and he's making tons of money. I'm not sure where I fit into this equation, except that I sound happy and available for sex.

When we're filling out paperwork in the waiting room, he leans over and asks, "What should my porn name be?"

"What?"

"Right here," says Joseph, pointing to his sheet of paper. "It asks for my 'stage name.'" This is an addendum to the typical medical release. Because we're at a clinic frequented mostly by porn stars.

"You don't even do porn," I tell him.

"But what if…"

"I don't care."

"It's supposed to be your first pet's name and the street you grew up on, right? So I'd be Catwoman Sixth. Not a good choice."

"You named your pet Catwoman?"

"It's funny, huh? What would yours be?"

I give in to the game. "Um, I guess I'd be Fluffy Mills. I grew up on Mills Lane…and had a rabbit."

"That's fucking great," says Joseph. "I should totally use that." He writes it on his paperwork.

Someone calls my name from behind a desk and I leave Joseph to his own amusement.

He says, "Best of luck," as I disappear into the medical establishment. Even though it means nothing, the boy sounds sincere.

71.

"Does this hurt?" asks the doctor, pushing a piece of cotton against my nose.

I flinch in accordance with my pain. "Yeah."

"It's definitely broken," he says, "and slightly off. We'll need to fix that."

"How do you mean, 'fix?'"

"You want a straight nose?" The doctor smiles. "Take a deep breath." He fingers my bridge and snaps it back into place.

My scream is psychologically muffled but it still comes out pretty loud. After a quick crunch, the throbbing spreads elsewhere. It's contagious; a head full of fire.

"I'd lay low for a couple days. Take it easy," he tells me.

"What if I have to work tomorrow?"

A shrug. "It's up to you. But like I said…" He hands me a prescription and some samples of Vicodin.

72.

Joseph peels a band-aid from his arm and crumples it on the diner table. He flicks it around like he's in a solo match of table tennis. "Jesus, they take…what? Three vials of blood? What's all that shit for?"

"HIV, Syphilis, and I don't know. It's to make sure you're clean."

"You scared?" he smirks.

"Not really," I say. "Everything's a gamble."

"My ass is worth it," he notes with pride.

I give him a reassuring nod because he's buying me lunch. And his ass is worth—if not "it"—something.

My ass vibrates. A text. I put the phone on the table and squint.

"Who's buzzing you?"

"My friend, Thad," I answer.

"He's in your band, right?"

"Uh huh." I'd totally forgotten about practice. According to Thad, I'm supposed to be in a warehouse, strumming loud chords. "Shit. I need to drop you off."

"Why? Just take me with you."

"You don't know where I'm going," I tell him.

"It doesn't matter." Then he goes, "Waitress!" and snaps his fingers above his head.

I pull his arm down and demand, "Stop it," in a hushed voice.

"Why?"

"Because it's rude. And stupid."

A young woman with an apron approaches. Joseph says, "You know I was joking, right?" Back to me, "Relax. She can take a joke."

The woman seems aloof.

"We need our food to go," says Joseph. "I was just playing around with the whole 'waitress' thing." He looks at me again. "It's a joke. I mean, I've always wanted to do that…"

73.

THAD HEADBANGS AND HOLDS DOWN some keys on his synth. I speed-pick notes and wait for the part where I'm supposed to scream. My mouth opens. Barely. Usually, my lips part wide and my face stretches like a lion. Today, the most basic enunciation makes me want to pass out. Every movement feels like tugging at the crack in my nose.

I stop strumming and swallow another Vicodin.

Thad follows suit except he's got no pills. "You sure you want to do this today?"

I go, "Uh."

Joseph is on the floor, stomach up. He's been staring at the ceiling and drumming his fingers along his ribcage while we practice. "I could try," he says. "I mean, it can't be that hard. All you have to do is sound like an animal. Everyone does that when they're kids. "

"Not quite," says Thad. He looks at me like, *Who is this guy?*

Joseph and I had been kind of vague about our relationship. Since we were an hour late, Thad didn't care to waste time with the explanation.

Unprompted, Joseph stands and walks towards my microphone. He taps it a bit, makes it feedback. "What are the lyrics?" he asks me.

My head's foggy, but I think I say, "They're not set in stone. Besides, I don't like speaking that stuff in a normal voice." Even less audible: "Not the right context."

"What's the song about?"

"Which one?" I ask.

"The one you were just playing."

"Oh. Um, death…and the unknown." I put down my guitar and say, "You don't have to…"

Joseph coughs in the microphone, then starts screaming.

When the kid stops, Thad nods in appreciation. "Not bad. You ever play in metal bands?"

"I've never played in any bands."

"Not bad," says Thad. Again.

"You guys want to try a song?" asks Joseph. "I'll feel it out, or whatever."

Thad looks at me and shrugs. "Your call, dude."

I pick up my guitar and Thad triggers the drums on his laptop. Joseph bounces around like some rock and roll caricature. But his voice screeches something close enough to scary black metal. I guess it sounds good, and I guess I'm happy that I don't have to do as much.

The song comes to an end and Joseph talks into the mic, his voice now raspy. "What do you think?"

Thad goes, "Cool." But Joseph only looks at me.

"Yeah, I'm into it," I say. "Just don't do that with your body."

"Why?" says Thad, like he's defending the kid. "It's different."

"Okay," I say. "I guess I'm just out of it." Even though I stand by my statement.

"How do you guys know each other?" asks Thad.

"We're roommates," answers Joseph. Without pause, he moves on to, "So am I in the band?"

I hold my face and sit down. "I need to go home."

74.

JOSEPH DRIVES US BACK TO my apartment, because I feel nauseous and I've swallowed too many pills. When he's about to park, he goes, "Oh shit."

"Huh?"

"I'm pretty sure that's my mom's car."

"Perfect," I tell him. "Let's say hi." Because I'm sort of fucked up, he probably thinks I'm joking. Maybe I am. But if Joseph's going to stay with me, I'd at least like to work out a shared custody situation.

"We should drive around a bit until she goes away. Or we could go out to lunch again. An early dinner."

"Joseph, my face hurts and I just want to crawl into bed."

"I'll pay for the dinner," he says.

"With your mom's money," I remind him. "That's probably why she's here."

He's braking a lot and turning on to random streets. "You should get out and I'll keep driving."

"Here?"

"I'll pull up to the apartment."

"I don't want to deal with your mom," I say. "She's not my problem."

"I love my mom," snaps Joseph. "She's not a problem."

"Then what the fuck?"

"I'm not in the mood," he says. "For her." His hand finds my thigh and rubs gently. "Please."

"Fine," I say. "But I'll probably make something up so she'll go away. It might be about you and it might not make things easier."

"Wait, what are you going to say?"

"I don't know. Just get me home."

"Okay." He removes his hand from my leg. "Left or right?"

"What?"

"I think I'm lost."

75.

GLORIA STANDS OUTSIDE MY FRONT door. She doesn't look happy.

"Where's Joseph!?"

"Roaming the streets, most likely." I say this while walking, but I don't get far. She holds me by the shoulders. I'm more than an arm's length from the door so I can't get a key in or even turn the handle. There's no energy in me to struggle. I tell her, "Let me go or I'll call the police."

She drops her arms and brushes the side of her pants. "Will you help me out here? I'm worried about my son. I know he's interested in you, but he needs…stability. Someone who will be there for him no matter what."

"Listen, we got in a fight. He ran off. I don't know where he is."

Some of her anger comes back, but she swallows it well. "Is he hurt?"

"I didn't do anything to him."

She motions to my nose. "Joseph hit you?"

I shrug and say, "I'm fine." Then I reach for the door.

Gloria blocks my path, but does her best not to touch me. "Wait. Can you at least do me a favor?"

My eyes roll, but the Vicodin makes everything sluggish. I hope she notices. "What?"

"Call me if he comes back here?" Gloria fumbles in her purse and pulls out a business card. "In case you lost my number." I'm unresponsive, so she adds, "I can pay you."

The last part's enticing. "How much?"

"I don't know. Twenty bucks?"

"Twenty bucks?"

"It's a phone call," she says. "You want more?"

As if I've taken to high ground. "I'm not a hooker about everything."

"That's not what I was suggesting. At all. But you want to be difficult? Fine. That's your right. You've done enough already."

"I fucking saved his life," I say, louder than anything else. "You said so."

She moves away from the door. "Right."

I search my pockets and realize the apartment key is with Joseph. There's no way inside unless I break something. It's a bad idea anyway. Given my current state, also impossible.

Because I'm just standing there, Gloria doesn't leave. "Do you have something to say?"

"No," I tell her, and lean my forehead against the wall.

"Your body language suggests otherwise."

"Oh my god, you're just like Joseph," I mutter.

This makes her smile and, unfortunately, go nowhere. "Is he inside?" asks Gloria, her voice now sweet and coaxing.

"No," I say. "I don't have my keys."

"Oh." Her tone shifts to petty disappointment. "Where are they?"

"Uhh…" I don't know why I'm covering for Joseph. She should take the kid back. That's what I want, right? Anything to the contrary isn't thought out, just reactionary. Still, I can't trust someone who will take their hands off me because I threaten to call some pigs. Joseph would probably hit me in the face again, which is honest. Also fucked up.

When my own rationale isn't making sense, it's because of something else. I might have feelings for the boy. It's complicated, but they're there. Most of the time I want him dead. But I'd rather not find out if I'd miss him.

"Come with me to the car. We'll call a locksmith." She adds, "I'll pay. No strings attached."

"That's not necessary." All I want is to lie down. Joseph's around the corner with the key. A locksmith might take an hour to get here.

"Do you have a phone on you?" she asks.

There's no weight in my pockets and my fingers find them empty. I must have left it in the car, too. "No." Or dropped it.

"Then you're coming with me." Gloria grabs me by the arm, but not too hard. "No police, okay? I'm not assaulting you."

"Please…" I croak as I'm dragged forward.

"Oh stop it," she says. "This isn't about Joseph."

76.

"Forty-five minutes?" Gloria looks at me, shrugs, says, "Okay," and then hangs up her phone. "You hungry?" she asks me.

I shake my head, "No."

"How about coffee?"

"No, thank you."

"We have some time to kill," she says. "There's a place down the street."

I walk beside her because I have nowhere else to go. Also, saying what I want might be the worst way to get it. I've at least caught on to that.

"Was this neighborhood your first choice?" asks Gloria. Everywhere she looks, she's frowning. "There *is* a lot of diversity."

"It's cheap."

"Hmm," she mouths. "I suppose I'd have lived here when I was younger."

When we get to the café, she orders something that sounds sweet but has the word *light* in front of it. She almost asks if I'd like a drink, but orders for me instead. My coffee tastes like chocolate and comes with whipped cream.

"How's work?"

I motion towards my bandaged nose. "Slow."

"Can I ask when he...when that happened?"

There seems no harm in telling her. "Last night."

"So he didn't stay with you? Did he say where he was going?" Before she ascends into panic, Gloria takes a deep breath. "I know it's not your problem...but did he?"

I've put myself in a corner, so all I've got for her is fiction. It is entertaining, however, to watch this woman get riled up. "He seemed angry. Like, he could do anything."

"What did you two fight about?"

"He was out in the street, screaming. That's the last I heard of him."

"Screaming at you?" She squints her eyes.

"Not necessarily," I tell her. "I thought we were fighting because I didn't want him to spend the night. After a while, it didn't seem like that's what he was upset about. He was saying all sorts of weird shit."

"What do you mean?"

"Ghosts, wraiths... I think he was seeing things, Gloria." I pause for effect. "Does your family have a history of mental illness?"

Gloria's eyes turn dead and she bites the air. "I know you're acting out because of some complicated trauma that far predates Ernest's...interference...in your life. But you are not my patient. So understand this. You can play these little games, fuck with me all you want. But if I find out you've harmed my son, there is no cop in this city who can protect you."

"Jesus," I say. "So he wasn't seeing ghosts."

"Where's my son?" she demands.

"I don't know."

Gloria uncaps my coffee and pours it in my lap. "Fuck you," she says, standing.

By the time I can think about cleaning myself up, she's outside. Gone.

77.

MY CROTCH IS DRY, BUT the stain makes it look like I shit my pants in a physiologically impossible way. Embarrassing. I look like a vagrant crashed out on my own front doorstep.

Some of the neighbors pass by and seem to recognize me. Not sure if it makes things better or worse. I mean for my self-esteem.

Eventually, Joseph shows up and asks, "What happened?"

I answer, "Your mom," which sounds like a frat boy joke and makes me hate my voice. So I just paw at the door and hope the gesture is obvious.

Joseph fumbles with the keys. "Sorry. I had to be sure she was gone…and I got lost again."

The door opens and I don't quite get to my feet. I think it's subconscious melodrama on my part, but the boy plays along. He crouches behind me, puts his arms under mine, and pulls me up by my chest. We limp forward until I fall on the bed and he falls on top of me.

"Thanks for dealing with my mom," Joseph whispers in my ear. "I swear I'll talk to her soon. Needs to be the right timing though, you know?" He rolls off me so that we can see each others eyes. "What did you two talk about?"

"She hates me." I let my eyes drop so I might steal some sleep.

"Don't say that. She doesn't even know you."

"It doesn't matter." I'm getting closer to the void.

"You know I appreciate it, right? Doing that for me. She can be a lot to handle, I know. That's why I need some time to get myself together. I need to be able to stand on my own two feet. Then I can tell her about all this. About us. She'll see it's a good thing." He strokes my face. "You're a good thing."

If it's a dream, my body interprets it as real. Joseph sits on top of me and rubs his hands along my back. My muscles come apart in his fingers. He slides from my neck and shoulders to the arch of my ass. His cock engorges in the slit between my cheeks. The tip rubs down and stops—hot against my hole.

The massage is paralyzing so I don't try to stop him. If it weren't for the knock at the door, the boy would be stretching my guts. I think, *Too bad the dream is over.* But I open my eyes only once. So it's more like, *Too bad nature didn't take its course.*

A unknown period of time passes and Joseph's back at my ear. "There's a locksmith at the door. He says you called him."

I think I nuzzle at Joseph. I think I want him to kiss me. The pressure of rubbing my face on anything is still excruciating, so I'm sure he's interpreting mixed signals.

"Should I let him in?"

I hear all of this but it doesn't mean I understand him. He's noise interrupting the fuzzy blackness on my eyes, the Rx dreams, the space between unfulfilled sex and nocturnal emissions. All of this mixed with the pain between my eyes.

Hands familiar enough to be mine—and they probably are—probe downwards, spreading and kneading skin. I try to find that comforting *push* from where we left off. Balance out the pressure, steal it from my broken face. I want to internalize the throbbing and play like I'm a girl. That's what I mean to tell him when I moan in his lap and stick three fingers up my ass.

"I'll be right back," says that voice again: a young man, breathy, impatient. He returns quickly, tripping over pants half-worn and caught at his ankles. His tongue washes my fingers and he shoves everything in my mouth. I taste our saliva together, and the musty sweat of my ass. Then another piece of foreign skin. The thing grows in my mouth and thrusts towards the back of my throat. With my hand still pressed against my tongue, the space is crowded. I'm choking, but in a way that makes me want to smile.

He pulls out of my mouth and hovers above me. I feel something in the air, like a question. So I open my eyes. Joseph's all shapes and soft lines. I can sort of tell he's naked.

"Can I be rough with you?" he asks. "Like you are with the girls?"

My answer isn't clear, but I feel him slap me anyways. He sees that I won't fight back, that I can't. The sounds I make must be good enough for him to continue.

By the time I'm getting fucked, I don't even notice. It's just another thing I can't process. But I think I'm happy. Definitely not sad.

78.

THE NIGHT IS EITHER LATE or fleeting. Our room is dark. Joseph's pressed against me as if we're habitually connected.

I roll on to my back and adjust my eyes to the shadows. It's enough to wake the boy.

"Are you asleep?" he asks me.

I shake my head, "No," but can't be sure he sees me.

Joseph moves inches closer and places his head on my chest. It's as if I've answered him and he's responded further. His thoughts drip into my lungs and I breathe them out before they reach my brain. Not on purpose. I've not yet learned to receive his telepathy.

"Sometimes I wish we were closer," says Joseph. In spoken words.

My hand is in his hair, holding a treasure. "How? We've ended up like this most nights since we met."

"Do you like it?"

I shrug, but then I squeeze him. His muscles flex into me. I say, "Yes."

"You probably think I'm naïve," he says. "That I don't get the difference between dreams and reality."

"What do you mean?"

"When I talk about us. I know you don't have to be my boyfriend and we might never grow old together."

"Have you talked about that?"

"See, you don't even listen. I already know that. At least, I'm not unaware of it. But I think you sometimes want to seem more distant than you are." His finger draws a line down my stomach. "Because you also lay here with me. Like this." He continues to paint my torso. It's less exploration now. More comfort. "I've never had a boyfriend."

Almost a laugh, because he sounds cute. Though I'm bleeding sincerity because it's late and I might actually be getting to know him. Might actually want to. "Neither have I."

"You've had girlfriends though. Like that girl my dad shot."

"She wasn't my girlfriend."

"I'm not replacing her?" he asks.

"No. I'm not sure what she was. Sometimes I forget that she existed, but that's probably my brain trying to deal with real life. I'm sure your mom could explain it."

"I don't think my mom's that good at explaining anything. She's too normal. I've heard you have to grow up depressed, or fucked up, to be a good shrink. Otherwise you look at your patients like they're freaks. You can't identify with them. I mean, look at my dad. She didn't see that coming."

"Can I ask?"

"What?"

"About your dad? Or... I mean, are you okay? Forget what he did to me. He was your dad. And...you know..."

"It's probably like with you and that girl," says Joseph. "I forget or I don't care. Or it's not real to me because I was in a coma...but I am concerned about his energy in the world. Even in jail, it has the ability to touch people. Some of them will get out. They'll put it back where the rest of us can get to it. And fuck... He writes letters. That's sending energy."

"What energy?"

"Think about a house where someone died. Not just died, but got murdered. People like to say it's haunted. It's not because of ghosts. It's energy. Think about how much fear and hate goes into something like that. Part of it has to remain. People pick up on that."

"You're saying that your dad's a haunted house?"

Joseph says, "Sort of. I remember when my parents split up. There was this pressure in his apartment. Everything felt heavy. I couldn't escape it... It obviously got worse. I can feel it on you sometimes."

"Maybe I'm haunted, too."

"Of course you are," he tells me. "It'll get worse if he keeps writing you. If you keep dwelling on it."

"I meant haunted for other reasons."

"No. I can feel the other part of you. Here." His hand is on my heart. It seems backwards, but I can sense his palm beating.

"What do you feel?" I ask him.

Joseph gets up and says, "Let's try something. Close your eyes. We can't touch." He sits a foot away from me, cross-legged. "Send me something special."

"Send how?"

"With your body, mind, whatever. And be open. I'll send you something, too."

I do as he says, and strike the same pose. I'm struck by silence and the sensation of being alone. It changes quickly. There's a moment of religious clarity. I've heard stories of people being held by God or angels. It must be something like this. There's a safety, then a purge. Water trickles down my face. Suddenly, I'm sobbing.

"What do you feel?" asks Joseph.

"I don't want to say." He must hear my choking, my staccato breath.

"Let it out. It's important."

"Okay." But it doesn't leave my tongue.

"I feel something from you," says Joseph.

"Okay." Again.

"It's like you love me."

"Wait, that's what I was going to say."

"That you love me?"

"No… I feel like it's more than that. But from you. You're in love with me."

"I am," says Joseph. "What do you feel about me?"

"It's like you said," I tell him. And I keep crying.

79.

THERE'S A PAUSE IN THE morning before we act like we always do. Joseph does whatever and I get annoyed, sort of turned on, then complacent. Maybe he feels differently. Because there's a gleam in his eye. Maybe he sees one in mine.

I don't acknowledge it because I have to go to work and I'm running behind.

"Let me make you breakfast," says Joseph.

"Not enough time," I say, rushing towards the exit.

"I'll come with you."

"Why?" We're both outside and I'm locking the door. Still arguing in the car. He tells me that we can stop somewhere on the way. A drive-thru. "No, no…" But I'm aware I need to eat. He says he'll pick me up something after I get to set. Like he's my personal assistant.

At work, I'm met with reprimand. "I can't shoot you like this," says the director. He means my broken nose and bruised eye sockets.

"Come on, man. Can't we work it into the story?"

"The story's been written. You think we make this shit up on the spot?"

I need the money bad. But the girl's also cute and the gender I'm supposed to be into. Smashing pussy would be good way to prove my ancient identity.

"I wish you'd told me about this earlier," says the director. "Now I need to get on the phone with the studio and figure out a replacement. *If* we can even shoot today."

"Sorry," I say. "I didn't think it would be a big deal."

The director's getting flustered and Joseph looks like he's concocting a plan. It's that smile I'm beginning to recognize. Means there's something about to leave his lips and it probably isn't helpful.

"I could do it."

"Who the fuck are you?" asks the director.

"Joseph," he says and tries to shake the director's hand.

"How many scenes have you done?"

Joseph hesitates and looks at me. "I don't know."

"'I don't know,' like you can't remember? I guess that's good." The director shouts, "Hey Lindsay!" and my should-be costar traipses in. "You know this guy?"

She looks at me and goes, "What happened to your nose?"

The director says, "The other one."

Lindsay shakes her head, "No."

"Would you fuck him?" he asks.

She shrugs. "Sure. I mean, is something wrong with him?"

"Is there?"

80.

HIS TEST COMES BACK CLEAN and he's available. So they give him a chance. I drag the boy outside to give him a pep talk. "It's hard," I say to Joseph. "You've never had to get your dick up on camera."

"How do you do it?" he asks.

I hand him a Viagra. He asks me if I can get him breakfast. "Anything is fine," he says. "As long as it's organic."

"You're gay," I remind him. "And she's a girl."

"But you gave me this." He holds up the blue pill. "So no problem, right?"

I'm dismissive because he doesn't get it. "You'll figure it out."

81.

AT WHOLE FOODS WITH MORE of Gloria's money because neither Joseph nor I have our own. I should be shopping at one of those week-old bins at the 99 Cents store. But I'm supposed to be giving Joseph the benefit of the doubt because he's trying. And I guess I'm, like, in love with him.

No worries. He'll pump through that girl and make the money for me (us). It's an affirmation he's told me to repeat. The longer I think on it, the less it comes out right. *"Who the fuck do you think you are?"* is an easier thought to get through my head.

"Is this organic?" I ask the nearest grocer.

"It should say on the packaging," she responds without stopping her work.

We can't afford this. To prove my point, I grab something more expensive than Joseph's packaged quinoa cakes. One of those local, cold-pressed juices with ten pounds of kale. He'll love that I'm hopping on his health-meme bandwagon.

After he inevitably fucks up his scene with the girl, I'll show him the receipt. Give him a lesson on the cost of living when one's incapable of useful work. Or any contribution to society. I've nailed down the lifestyle. It's called getting by. Supplementing income with an excess of time and fame—the kind no one cares for.

I've given myself to the cause. Not an important one. The junk mail of careers. Anyone willing to look at the fine print would laugh. For whatever reason, Joseph's still finds it worthwhile. I should be thankful, right? Better than a *friend* who tries to save me.

"You get good at this. Take some of the load off," I'll say. "You want to be my sugar daddy? I'll have more time to rot."

I can't bring myself to actually feel this way. Porn is my thing. The one part of me I can still call *punk*. Everyone thinks they get it, but they don't. Take that away from me. Move along in my place. Once again, Joseph, "Who the fuck do you think you are?"

82.

I LET MYSELF BACK IN to the shoot location without a knock. They might be in the middle of filming. True to my suspicions, I find studio lights and naked bodies on a couch.

It's how I imagined. Joseph's face is red and he's pulling limp meat. The girl's on her knees, acting helpful but not doing much. The director's pacing and then not.

When he sees me, the director rolls his eyes. He walks over. "Where'd you find this kid?"

"Can I have a minute with him?" I ask.

"You know it's over," he says. "I'm not even trying to be fair at this point. Just cooling down so I don't kill someone."

"You're probably right. But I'd still like a minute."

"Oh yeah, help yourself." It's all sarcasm. "By the way, I'm blaming this half on you."

I ignore him and make my way to Joseph. The boy opens his eyes just in time to find me standing over him. "Hey." He smiles like I caught him in the cookie jar.

"With me," I tell Joseph and drag the boy towards the bathroom. Once the door is closed and locked, I say, "See?"

"Your Viagra didn't work."

"No," I respond. "Your head didn't work. The pill doesn't help you get it up. It just helps you keep it. Plus, you don't like pussy."

"I haven't even tried it yet."

"You might like pussy?"

He shrugs. Then starts kissing me. "Help me out a little."

My tongue goes in his mouth. But I break it up so I can say, "The director's already pissed. Let's cut our losses. He might still hire me in the future."

"It's working," says Joseph. He puts my hand between his legs and I feel him swell.

"Because I'm working," I remind him.

"Stand where I can see you. If I'm fucking up... Instead of her, I'll look at you."

"You're fucking stupid," I say and bite his lip.

Except it works.

The girl's ego might be falling off a cliff. At least she looks unsettled when we come out of the bathroom together and Joseph's sporting an erection.

The director doesn't care. "Stick it in her mouth. Let's do this!"

I hang out and watch. Joseph occasionally shifts his eyes to me. He holds his stare until I flash him a few strokes of my cock. Then he's back to pounding the girl in front of him. The boy even smiles when he pops on her face. It's a proud moment. For both of us.

83.

"It doesn't feel the same, but I'd call it 'comforting,'" says Joseph. "Like I didn't want to stop."

"You think you can do it again?" I ask.

"If you're there, sure. If not..." He takes a moment. "I can probably learn. It seems like something you have to learn."

"Pussy or porn?"

"Both."

"I don't know," I tell him. "Like, I can't believe you actually did it. So congratulations. But maybe you should try gay porn."

"Maybe later," he says. "Then I'll be unstoppable."

84.

I CHECK THE MAIL BACK at home. There's another letter from Ernest.

Joseph eyes it and gets a big ol' grin. He pulls the envelope from my hands. "Let's read it together," he says, running towards the bedroom.

I take my time and stroll in behind him. When I see the boy on the bed, he comes off as manic and then slightly depressed. One of those roller coasters of facial expressions and breath.

"Fuck, I can't wait to get my hands on him," says Joseph.

"What do you mean?" I ask and sit beside him.

The boy goes, "You remember our plan," to which I nod. Not quite sure what he means, but I recall an offhand remark about Joseph killing Ernest. I still can't take it seriously.

Joseph flattens the pages out on his lap and then folds them up again. "Maybe we should celebrate first," he suggests.

"Celebrate what?"

"That I'm a porn star! Aren't you proud of me?"

"I already told you."

"No you didn't." He frowns.

"I'm proud of you," I tell him.

"Squish me."

"What?"

Joseph lays on his back and tells me to get on top of him. "Just put all of your weight on me."

I put my hands and feet in the air so I'm no longer supporting myself. My body presses Joseph's into the bed. He makes funny faces, kisses me, then says, "I love this."

"Good." I smile, and feel weak despite the fact that I'm crushing him "How do you want to celebrate?"

85.

JOSEPH HAS ME DRIVE HIM to a liquor store outside of our neighborhood. He tells me to wait in the car.

"I'm over twenty-one," I remind him.

"You asked me how I wanted to celebrate, right?"

I nod.

"This is part of it. I feel…good…and I don't want it to stop." Before he runs inside, the boy turns and motions for me to roll down the window. "Keep the car running!"

I thought it was weird to begin with. Now I'm sure he's robbing the place. It doesn't bother me as much as it should. In fact, I don't protest at all. I mean, the boy's done something good for once. Instead of blowing the money he made at work, he's being creative. I have to admire it.

My hands tremble because my body's picked up on the danger. I'm an accomplice, the get-away driver. It's the most interesting role I've played since I moved to Los Angeles.

I wish Sara could see this, I think and don't know why. It almost brings me down. She might be happy for me in general. But if she was a sacrifice to get me a few new kicks, maybe not. Now I'm stuck on the fact that I don't know what her life was about at all. Not apart from me. She was cool to hang out with and she wanted to fuck me. Then she died.

And what about Joseph? I haven't tried to figure him out either. Because he watched my videos and jerked off, I thought his life was about me. Not entirely. Though on some unconscious level, I made the connection. Must have felt it was true.

But it's not. He keeps doing stuff that I don't understand and I usually hate it. Until he fills me up or wraps his guts around me. Then I get addicted. I tell myself he's bad and I still keep going. That's the way it works.

Except I'm starting to recognize a different kind of pattern. Forward momentum. Change. Every day with the boy is a new kind of scary. But it's not a downward spiral. It doesn't always get worse. The wool could be pulled so far in front of my eyes that I can't see at all. Or Joseph could be breaking me down for the better. Revealing a higher path.

Like, why steal when he can afford it? The boy's not desperate, just trying to get off. Maybe it's also a lesson. For me. Not everything in life can be worked for. Sometimes it has to be taken—at someone else's expense.

Joseph runs out of the store with a bulge of bottles in his pants. The *gangster* thing isn't pulled off well. His style's all about form-fitting clothes, hipster jeans, and Chuck Taylors. That fucking smile though—cute.

I open the door for him so he doesn't lose a second to the angry shopkeeper on his tail. Joseph jumps in and waves goodbye.

We're off into the night. Characters. Archetypes. Criminals in love.

86.

WE GET FUCKED UP AND then just fuck. Forget about Ernest's letter long enough that it's lost in the sheets, covered in sweat and alcohol. When we find it, the ink is smeared. Though we piece it together. Or most of it. Between the two of us.

"It looks like, 'Dear Danny.'"

"Yeah, no shit."

Laughter. "Okay, continue."

87.

Dear Danny,

Still no response. Perhaps you're not capable of writing back. Must I make myself clear before such a thing is possible? Yes, I understand. I've not revealed everything.

Sometimes I do my best to imagine myself as you. Like an ant pictures itself a dog. Even so, I sense confusion.

I've mentioned my ritual several times now. "Why a ritual?" you may ask. "What use is that?"

Great minds say we've entered a post-secular age. Those with any sense will not call upon the gods and expect a reply. We'll not pray as if we're communicating with the divine. But we'll still pray.

Mysticism will seep into our lives and culture. Many times in ways we don't understand. Thus, the ritual is not lost. It is an important process because it's always been an important process. If nothing else, it transforms us from one state to another.

The old mystics were wise beyond their years. They facilitated transformations for the normal and average, even the nearly excellent. When it comes to sex, Danny, who should I call upon but a seasoned slut for hire?

Now think of my ritual. It needs a purpose. I'm old and dying, and need not go further in life lest I perform the ritual of death. Mine was to take me back in time. Except it had nothing to do with time. Only regression. Innocence. A place where fantasy might still relate to health.

Think of the kids who shoot up their schools. Before they commit the act, the idea is not so bad. Who of us has not thought about killing our boss, neighbor, friend, or partner? There's always one in life to piss us off and an imagined world where he is ripped apart. Most keep it in the head. As you know, I did not.

When we talk of innocence, it is not only the difference between acting and not. The definition is arbitrary. All it requires is a common starting point. We are all born and believed innocent at birth. However, a great deal of children come into the world screaming. A doctor slaps them on the ass to draw breath. Immediately, the child knows hate. It's not so complex a feeling.

If you disagree with my assessment, think of when the child is dressed. In this country, a mother goes to the store and buys the cheapest outfit for her infant. Perhaps one with a cute button that costs a few dollars more. In all likelihood, the outfit is cheap because it was produced by a child. In some other country far away. For little or no pay. In terrible conditions. Something we like to call abhorrent.

The infant did not choose to buy the outfit. But it is warm and comfortable as a result of suffering. Is the infant innocent through and through? It survives and something else dies. Even at birth, it gives its mother pain.

We've all been there, so we call it innocence. But it's a simple commonality. The more we digress from one another, the more we're able to cast blame. Some may be appropriate. After all, I blame myself. That is why I set this thing in motion. A man cannot live so far from the rest. It hurts too deeply. I had to make my way back to common ground.

Imagine if I told my wife how I'd fucked our son. What would be her response? Nothing good, I'm sure. But if she had fucked him, too? If she'd even sucked his cock? Perhaps we'd share our exploits. As if one had taken Joseph to ice cream, and the other to pizza. "Yes, he ordered chocolate," or, "We shared a large triple-cheese. It was wonderful."

If my wife is such a parent, I don't know. In the past, I couldn't risk to ask her. Now it doesn't matter. After I'd taken Joseph, I longed for such a wife. Then I realized she needn't be a wife. Or even mine.

When a man drinks the blood of Christ and eats his flesh, it's just crackers and wine. Still, the experience is profound. It's the feeling one has of communion with God.

You are not my wife, Danny. Thankfully, you are no woman at all. But your gift allows you to be whatever is needed. Don a red dress and you become both my wife and the thing she must represent. Red Riding Hood. Something like innocence and bravery. Also, my savior and punishment. Maybe everything.

When you took Joseph in your mouth, I masturbated myself with great relief. I can't even explain. Her essence was in you. You channeled this thing without even knowing it. You said nothing terrible to me. You asked nothing about my force. Once into the act, you sucked until completion. The seed in your mouth brought you to my level, and regressed me into yours. We shared something. A commonality. We were back to beginning and no one could tell us we were wrong.

Of course, I could never reach the place where you reside. You've done this so many times in so many different ways. It was you, as my Gloria Brown, who did this thing.

Did you understand it at the time? That you had become my strongest familial bond? Surely not. But you knew the purpose was outside of you. A true holy man of our time. You bear the weight of our burdened sex. Whether we want an old woman, a young cunt, or the reunion of a wife and son.

Forgive me if I took drastic measures to add my burden to the rest. I'd been studying you for years and had great feelings of your capability. If I didn't believe you able, I would have found someone else. Please believe me. Because I believe in you.

I believe you're out there, thinking no great deal of my conflict. Is that why you don't reply? It means hardly a thing to you? Surely, you carry on with misunderstood strength.

That is why I must write you. I couldn't stand long enough to pay the money you deserve. So I must explain your worth in other ways.

What you've done means a great deal to me. Yes, it stands incomplete. Because I did not last long enough to share my psychological state. But you performed the physical act and it was almost enough. At least for me.

Don't misunderstand. I know the ritual is a symbolic thing. My transgressions remain whole and true. The wolf must be slaughtered. It's the nature of the story. Though without a story, I am less than a wolf. Just a dying man.

Take away my needs and you've still done your part, Danny. You've come through. So ask anything of me. I'll vouch for you. To the public, to whomever you want.

Your friend and admirer,

Ernest Brown

88.

"What should we ask him?" says Joseph, slurred.

"I don't understand the question."

"He says right there…'ask anything of me.'"

"Fuck your dad," I say.

"Obviously. But… If I didn't want to do it myself, I'd ask for suicide."

"It's not your decision."

"I'm a victim of rape," he says like it's supposed to be funny.

"Do you feel like you've been raped?" I ask.

"What?"

"Do you feel like you've been raped?"

"By Ernest or you?"

"In general…and he's no longer 'Dad?'"

Joseph starts crying, but nothing else about him looks sad. His face doesn't change. No difference in posture.

"Why are you crying?" I ask.

"I should be able to remember. To own it."

I move in closer because I feel like I should console him. "It would probably be worse. Maybe you should be, like, grateful."

"I'm not grateful."

"Okay," I say, and hug him. "I'm sorry."

He whispers, "Is it true what he said? That you can become someone else? For sex?"

"I don't know."

"Could you be my dad?"

There's distance between us now. I've made it. "Fuck your dad."

"That's what I want. To fuck my dad." Another line of water from his eye. "And not want it."

"I lied. I do know the answer. 'No.' I can't become someone else."

"Let's go to bed," he says and lays down on his stomach. Spreads his ass.

"I don't feel like having sex right now," I say.

"Ernest's full of shit."

A part of me that can't be touched feels punctured and bled dry.

"Obviously."

89.

THE MORNING MAKES US FORGET the night before. If not forget, acknowledge nothing. We're back to thoughts of breakfast, Facebook, and how to survive.

By the time I'm awake, Joseph's eaten his cereal. The bowl has traces of milk and sits next to my computer. Joseph is in front of it. He talks to the screen.

Thad talks back. "I think we're trying to channel darkness. There's nothing specific. So I think you can interpret that however you want."

"I was looking at my Facebook feed this morning," answers Joseph. "I saw this meme on the nutritional content of GMO corn versus organic corn. There's no comparison. The GMO stuff has almost nothing. It reminds me of a documentary I watched on how there are these people, not even in the government, but above it. Like Illuminati. They're concerned with overpopulation so they've put this stuff in our food and water to slowly kill us off. Have you heard of fluoridated water? Or fucking toothpaste? Everyone knows about that. Well, sodium flouride is the same shit they use in rat poison."

"We're not really a political band," says Thad.

"I just turned eighteen. I've never voted. How the fuck can I be political? I'm talking about mass extinction," says Joseph. "What's darker than that?"

"Fuck man, that sounds crazy."

"Right? I'll talk to Chris about the deadline."

"It's not really a deadline. But you know…Without a goal, it's hard to make shit happen."

"What shit?" I ask. I'm no longer pretending to be asleep.

"Hey dude," says Thad.

"Are you on my Skype account?" This is me to Joseph.

"It was open already. Thad called me 'cause he thought it was you."

"Oh."

"We're talking about the recording," says Joseph. "Your friend's got ideas. For lyrics and stuff."

"Did we decide to record?" Because I don't think we did.

"Yeah. And relax. It's cheaper with another person in the band."

"Cool," I say and leave them for my own bowl of cereal.

Joseph joins me in the kitchen minutes later. "How do I get more work?" he asks.

"I don't know." Between spoonfuls, "I guess you need an agent."

"Do you have an agent?"

"Not anymore."

"But you used to?"

"Yeah."

"So how do I get an agent?"

I smile a certain way that Joseph doesn't like. Because he says, "Don't do that. I know what it means when you smile like that. It means you think I've said something stupid."

"Oh come on," I say. "You want an agent? Who's gonna take you? You haven't done anything."

"Fuck off. I've done something." He's not quite mad, not quite joking.

"The scene's not out. And who's gonna vouch for you? The director? The girl? You nearly bombed."

"But I didn't. And you can vouch for me."

"Me?"

"Why not?" asks Joseph.

"Because… I don't know. Who am I?"

"You're fucking 'Danny Wylde.' Own that shit." He refrains from the usual physical contact, which is weird and almost coaxing. "Just give me a number and your name as a reference. And if they want to talk to you… I can put you on the phone, right?"

I shrug.

"Give me a fucking chance." The boy pouts. From his drooping face comes something motivational. "We have to be a team or this turns into a nightmare. Trust me, help me, have a little faith. I mean, come to the shoots if you have to. Make out with me in the bathroom. If that's what it takes…" He's a public speaker in my kitchen. Lit with enough energy and charisma to tip me over the fence. I fall on the better side of apathy.

"If it doesn't work out, you have to find something else. Okay?"

"Yeah, of course," he says with kisses and thank yous. I remind the boy that nothing's happened. He picks up the phone and says, "Wait and see."

90.

Joseph's dream is contagious. Not that other people want the same thing. He just gets them on board with making his shit happen. The agency caves in minutes and it's only the first number I give him. Yeah, I talk on the phone a bit. I say good things about the boy. That's part of his charm too. I get off on seeing him happy.

Within the first week, he lands two jobs. Because my face is still healing, I hand him a third. All little pieces of the porno pie. The pay is terrible by veteran standards, but it's better than minimum-wage or anything else he could manage as a blossoming high school dropout.

I say I'm his driver, friend, or the guy helping him out. Most of the crews recognize me so it's no big deal that I hang around on set. When Joseph's about to get into sex, I slip into the bathroom and suck his cock. Then he rushes out in front of the lens and fucks like a straight kid.

We do something nice and couple-like after each victory. Go out to dinner or look at clothes he'd buy if the cash flow were heavier. He stares at me and dreams out loud. He says, "It isn't enough. We have to do more." Then we find the cheapest way to get stoned, drunk, or fill an adrenaline rush. Some of the clothes he'd like to buy come home with us for free.

"I want you to break in these pants," says Joseph. "Look at this rich-people bullshit. I want to be rich, but always at our level. We have to make it dirrrrty." He drags the word out needlessly. Like a club girl trying to be *hood*. "I'm almost too tired to fuck. You can jerk off on them. Or if you're too tired, take a piss."

We get in the bathtub. I laugh as my stream soaks his designer jeans. It's hard to control a piss when things are funny. So it's harder when his face gets hit with urine.

It's good that he laughs, too. And swallows. If we're to become a team, our mutual consumption of each other surely helps. The myths of cannibals who obtain powers through what they eat must be partially true for the stuff that comes out of the body: cum, spit, piss.

I feel less worthless after tonguing Joseph's ass. There's something in there that doesn't taste like shit. It's positive vibes and some proper ignorance. Because I'm thinking, "Life's not so bad."

91.

THE BRUISES AROUND MY EYES start to match the color of my skin. I make some calls. Get back to my own work.

"Do you want me to come with you?" asks Joseph.

"It's cool," I tell him. "I was doing this way before I met you."

"Can I come anyways?"

"I don't think so." I've been waiting for this, secretly. Autonomy. The power to do things on my own. Though mostly pussy. The warm and snug place that used to be my favorite. It was taken from me in a variety of ways. One of which used to be the over-availability that comes with the job. When a favorite thing becomes a necessity, it's no longer a favorite thing. But I've had some time off and expanded my taste. I don't want to be reminded of Joseph when I reenter the fray.

92.

HER NAME WAS LEFT OFF the call sheet. So it's a surprise to see her here, getting painted in the makeup chair. "Danny!" she says. We hug. Tighter than I would most girls on set.

I saw her last in a videotaped orgy. We'd spent too much time together and I was asked to cum on someone else. Still, I looked at her to make myself get there.

"Hey Rachel. How've you been?"

"Good," and, "You know, the same," are the first things she tells me. Because it's necessary and common form. Then a few hours go by because someone fucked up the schedule and shoots always involve waiting around.

Rachel mentions a boyfriend I've probably been introduced to. But I don't remember. She says he's doing better.

"Better than what?"

"He was in a really dark place last year. He didn't have a job. Because I was bringing in all the money, he felt even worse about it. There were a lot of drugs around the house."

"How did he pay for the drugs?" I ask.

She looks at me like it's obvious and I'm an asshole for asking. "He's working for a good company now. In a few years he could be making forty bucks an hour. Then maybe I can quit all this. His company… They have a branch in San Diego. That's where I want to start my little café on the beach."

"Sounds wonderful. I'd love to buy a cup of your coffee."

Rachel smiles and tells me, "You will." Then her forehead scrunches up and the smile's gone. "There's such a long road to get there. I need at least thirty thousand for a down payment on something like that. I have debts. I have to pay off my car. This used to be fun when I first got in, but I enjoy running errands more than going to work. My body's tired." She adds, "I'm tired."

"I get it," I say, which is my way of empathizing despite the fact that I am the work.

"Didn't mean to bum you out. Sometimes I have fun. When I found out I was working with you…that made me feel better."

"No one told me. But I was pretty happy to see you. I mean, I am happy." I look at her and she holds my stare for a while.

"I used to have such a crush on you. You know that? Then you stopped answering my calls. Did you change your number because of me?"

"I didn't change my number."

"Funny." She plays it off as her mistake, but I can tell she believes it's mine.

"I still have a crush on you," I say. For the moment, it's true. "As much as I can given the circumstances."

There was a time she could have been my girlfriend. We spent thirteen hours on set and she came home with me. The next day we played miniature golf. I won a pair of oversized sunglasses in the arcade, which I gave to her. They ended up in the trash.

There wasn't a fight or a point where it fell apart. I mean, the chemicals in our bodies needed each other. That much was obvious. But after a few days—maybe a week—I couldn't speak to her. I didn't know how. There was something else in my life. That was my excuse. An invisible force that kept me from experiencing her. I made it sound as if it swallowed up my time. As if it were an activity I attended to every day.

The truth was I'd come home and sit by myself. Fifteen minutes would pass and I'd enter a state of mourning. I'd pick up the phone and mean to call her. But I wouldn't. Eventually, I'd stop feeling bad and move on to something else: camming, videogames, sleep.

Later, I said we had nothing in common. That it couldn't be helped. A year passed and she got over the way I behaved. We'd start to notice each other on set. Always, we found something to talk about. Never what happened or what could have been. Only nice, flirtatious things. Sometimes it would lead to our own filmed sex. It would be better than anything we'd had in months.

"I'm sorry," I tell her now. "I met you at a weird time in my life." It feels honest when it comes out. Maybe the time spans my entire existence. The fact that I came across her at all makes it true.

"I know it's for the best. My boyfriend…" She pauses. "He wants to treat me like a princess. All I've ever wanted is to be a princess. Is that too much to ask for?" If she's leaking, I don't see it. But she wipes a finger under her eye, sniffles, and then takes a deep breath. "I can't fuck up my makeup."

"I don't know what to say except I'm happy things are working out for you."

Rachel brightens slowly. "What about you? Are you seeing anyone."

"Not really," I say.

"Oh. I heard things. Just rumors, I guess."

"What did you hear?" I'm almost positive no one knows about Joseph.

"Someone said… It was a while ago. But they said you were seeing Sara. I forget her last name."

"Oh." And then, "Yeah, I guess it's just rumors."

"Did you hear about…? Wait, maybe it's the same Sara. Anyway, I heard about this porn girl who died. She wasn't working much anymore. I think her name was Sara."

If memories were words, this one would be on the tip of my tongue. I do my best not to let it fall off. Too late for the feeling though. The lump in my throat moves down.

"Yeah, I heard about something like that."

"So much for our image, right?" says Rachel. "People think we're all on our way to suicide. That girl was probably into some bad shit. Nothing to do with porno."

"What do you know about it?" I try to sound curious but come off angry. As if I stand in defense of the dead.

"Nothing. I'm just saying it sucks when I'm trying to do my best and these crazy bitches keep fulfilling the stereotype."

"It could have been an accident. Normal people die, too."

"I'm not trying to argue with you. But I heard she got shot. Maybe that's more normal than I'd like to admit, but it sounds like some bad shit."

I close my eyes and shrug. "Guess we'll never know." To try and change the subject, I add, "God, you look cute."

The image of her is stolen from the past. With chopped up hair and high school goth makeup. Before she got into money and became a true porn star. When I open my eyes, she looks tired and a little too tan. Still cute. Still trying to figure me out.

"You never call girls sexy or hot, huh? I remember that about you."

"I didn't know that was something about me. But I guess you're right."

"It's not exactly unique. Just not the usual from guys I'm about to fuck for money."

"What does your boyfriend say?"

There's something sincere in her shift of energy. Happiness at the thought the boy back home. "He's shy with words," says Rachel. "So he writes me letters."

I ride her vibe and say, "I guess things turned out the way the way they were supposed to."

She nods and then caters to the needs of a photographer. The man rifles through her belongings and asks her to try on a few outfits.

Fifteen minutes later, we're fucking. Rachel and I hold ourselves together for the seconds we can buy before opening up for the camera. She says, "I love your cock," for the shotgun mic pointed at her mouth. With her face hidden behind my neck, it's just, "I love you."

Cum hits her face like in every other porn film. I stand above. Rachel below. An end to the best sex I've had on camera since the last time we fucked.

A camera flash captures the moment before my erection falls. Then Rachel stands and stumbles away. "See you around," she says as a bathroom door cuts off a syllable.

I get dressed and make sure I'm gone before she's done with her shower.

93.

THERE'S A HOLE IN ME left by the scene. It makes me want to tell Joseph how necessary he is in my life.

I need it to sound moving. Or at least clever. That's what I try to come up with on the way home. Maybe I have it stored in my brain. But it falls apart when I hear him shouting from the other side of our apartment door.

"I'm taking your advice!"

A woman's voice matches his in tone and volume. "I lose you for two years and then you run away from home and…and that's somehow taking my advice?" Definitely Gloria.

"How can I run away from home when I live here?"

This goes on for several minutes while I stand still. Eventually, the voices fall to a level where words are inaudible. So I knock.

There's silence. I knock again. This time, footsteps move in my direction.

Joseph opens the door. He appears in a state between terror and relief. "Chris, I…"

Gloria eyes me from the kitchen and cuts off her son. "Good, you're here. You, of all people, should know how inappropriate this is."

Joseph turns around and shouts, "He makes me fucking happy, Mom! How do I get that through your stupid skull?"

"Joseph!" Gloria's face tightens and she averts her eyes to the floor. There's a long pause. Maybe to blow off steam. When she's back, her words attack me. "You want to deal with this? You think you have the tools to deal with this? Right now? With your lifestyle?"

"Um," I say as Joseph grabs my arm. "Yeah."

"We're adults," says Joseph. "We can do what we want."

"You're stealing money from me," bites Gloria. "You can't even support yourself."

"I told you I'd pay you back. I have a job now."

"Selling your body is not a job."

"Lady, I don't know what you're doing in my apartment…" I say to Gloria.

"Oh, you don't know, huh?" She gets closer to my face.

"I'd like you to leave."

"He's my son. Joseph is my son!" Gloria tries to grab on to the boy, but he bats her away. Within seconds, she's sobbing. "This isn't fair."

I open the door and allow her the space to walk through it. She doesn't budge.

"It's not like I'm divorcing you as a parent," says Joseph. He's now as sweet as he can muster.

"Joseph, you are my flesh and blood. You've been through so much and I only want what's best for you. I will not let you throw your life away..." My body flinches because it looks like she's winding up to kill me. "I will fight for you."

"You're so dramatic," says Joseph. He hugs his mother and she clings to him like a child.

I'm no longer as irritated by the situation because Gloria seems so awkward in the way she's falling apart. I'd still rather see her leave than continue her train wreck in my apartment.

"Listen, we'll visit you, or something," I tell her. "But tonight we have, um, plans."

Joseph pulls me into a group hug. Then provides momentum for baby steps towards the door.

Gloria doesn't seem to notice that she's outside in the hall. Her eyes are closed as she receives a kiss from her son. I say, "Bye." She makes a retching noise. Joseph retreats into the apartment before I shut the door.

"I'm not sure I know how to handle that," I whisper, and kind of slide to the floor.

"Oh my god, you're amazing," says Joseph. "I can't believe you didn't get mad."

"She's harmless, right?"

The boy tries to crawl in my lap but we're mostly just a pile on the floor. "Yeah. And besides, I'm here to protect you."

"I came home with this idea and I forgot how to make it sound good. The point was...is...that you're important to me. I just want you to know that."

"That's what you were thinking about today?"

I kiss him in reply and think, "This is what normal people must feel like together."

"Most people who meet their idols get let down," says Joseph. "But you're more my hero now than ever."

"Why?" I ask.

"Because..." Joseph needs a minute to think about it. "Everything about you makes sense. Like, people out there on the internet and stuff… They think you have these strange motivations. People like my dad. But I don't think that's true." He plays with my hair. "You want to go out and fuck whoever you want. You want to make money. And you want to come home to someone who loves you"

"Is that all you think about me?" Because I don't know how to take it.

"Don't be like that. I'm not trying to define you. I'm telling you that I like how everyone…okay, I mean people like me… in the past… Those people think you're a god. But you're just normal and like to fuck. Maybe you're better at fucking than most people. Whatever. Now you're mine."

"That doesn't sound heroic," I say, though I'm not upset. "Do you know what I like about you?"

"What?"

"I guess it's more about how I feel. Before I met you, I knew exactly how every day would go. At least the gist of it. I couldn't even want things to be different because then everything would fall apart. But now it's not like that. I'm alive, so I guess everything hasn't fallen apart. I don't know what's going to happen next, but that's actually exciting. Or maybe scary. In a good way. And yeah, I like coming home to someone who loves me."

"Guess what I also like?"

"Huh?"

"You're willing to deal with a crazy person so you can have another crazy person. Because I'm worth it."

"Your mom?" I gather.

"And me," says Joseph.

"Okay, me too."

94.

THE UNIVERSE ALLOWS US AN interesting schedule. For about a month. I'm always free when Joseph gets a job. I can drive him and prep the boy to fuck. On the days I'm paid to sling dick, Joseph's in the mood to write lyrics and practice his black metal voice. Or decorate the apartment.

Financially speaking, there are less problems. Familiarity grows between us. We attain some emotional symbiosis. If our cocks could think: "This is as good as it gets."

About six weeks in, an experiment comes our way. We get double booked. I don't want to cancel my job and Joseph needs to show up to everything he's offered. So we give it a try.

"Tell your agency you need a driver," I say to Joseph. "'Cause I'm using my car."

He figures it out and I go to work.

95.

MY SCENE IS WITH A Latin MILF whose pussy tastes like candy. I'm not sure if it's lathered with lotion or she's a good kind of diabetic. But the effect is tasteful and I spend a lot of time chewing her hole. The thing is extra wet when I'm invited in.

She smiles mostly and says all the right porno shit. But she pulls at my hand more than a few times while it's clasped around her neck. I whisper, "Sorry, my boyfriend likes to pass out on my dick. It's a habit."

"You're a faggot?" she says, louder.

The director stops rolling and goes, "What's the problem?"

"He's talking about choking his boyfriend."

"I think you misunderstood," I say. Still thrusting.

The MILF's not running away, but her eyes are angry and she's calling me out. "Motherfucker, I heard you."

"Look, my dick is in you. I'm not a fag."

At that, her pussy slides off me. "Repeat what you said."

"Dude, what did you say?" Now the director's ganging up on me.

"I don't know," I stutter. "Something about my girlfriend, I guess."

"Who's your girlfriend?" asks the MILF. Because I don't answer quick enough (or at all), she yaps, "See!"

The director changes sides. "I've shot Danny a bunch of times and I'm pretty sure he's not gay."

"'Sure' based on what?"

"For one, he fucks girls for a living."

She calms down a little, but has to make her point. "Listen, I've got nothing against gay people. But a lot of 'em got AIDS. It's just statistics."

I mutter "Oh my god," under my breath and keep it there. Because there's still room to salvage this and maybe get paid.

"You saw his test," says the director. "No HIV. So definitely no AIDS."

Her eyes lock on mine and they continue to search. "You swear to Christ you just slipped your tongue about a boyfriend?"

"Yeah. I mean, I don't think I said 'boyfriend.'"

"Plus he already fucked you," says the director. "He can't unfuck you. We might as well finish the scene, right?"

"Fine."

96.

FLUSHED RED BECAUSE I'VE HAD to drag myself through borderline-hostile cunt with the help of a few extra boner pharmaceuticals. But I have a check and I'm home—with a headache.

Joseph's missing, which I hope means he's in the midst of a good job.

I sprawl out on the bed with the concept of missing him. Like it's something romantic. But the sound of pure city noise suddenly seems quiet. Peaceful. No talking or sucking, or mentions of Facebook.

To think of what to do with my freedom is a burden. I could sleep or jerk off. Except that's what I'd do anyways. The context would only shift to cuddle and fuck.

My eyes track around the room. A bookshelf with pages that once held my interest. An instrument on the floor. In theory, I still know how to play it. My computer. Nothing useful. Just distractions.

What would I be if I was actually left alone with myself? I mean for longer than a day or week. Without depression or the post-traumatic stress of someone's death. As of now, the instinct to rub my cock and zone out is all there is.

Not like there's been enough time to figure out the answer. I just wonder if maybe Ernest is right. At least what I understand him to mean. That I'm this thing that gets hard and people can project on. Anything they want.

In movies, I'm sure it's true. But in real life? Is there a reason I'm perfect for it? I feel like I'm interesting because I can think about it. Though that doesn't mean much when I don't actually want to do anything interesting.

I don't want to get up. I don't want to learn. And I don't want to make something new. I just want to wait for Joseph to come home and make things…exciting. Like I told him before.

Maybe that's the proof we're meant to be together. He found me and projected love. Beyond that, I'm a plastic void. Filtering erectile dysfunction drugs. Embracing the fantasies of men with money. Giving it to kids who know how to steal just about everything.

97.

JOSEPH WAKES ME FROM A daydream. He doesn't look upset.

I kiss him and say, "It went well?"

"I think so," he tells me. Then confirms it for at least one of us. "Yeah."

"Look at you, all beaming." Empathy wakes me further until I realize it's something else. Still, I say, "I'm happy for you. Really."

"Don't get me wrong," he says. "It's cool to know I might be good at this. But the other guys confuse me. The performers, I mean."

"How so?"

"It was a gangbang. So there were about six of us. *Perfect for me,* I thought. You know, in case the girl was gross. Anyway, they were all talking. And I was mostly nodding and stuff. One of them told a story about a friend he had in high school. The point was that he found a jar of vaseline in his friend's bag; along with a fresh pair of underwear. He called his friend a fag and left him on the side of the road. They never spoke again."

"Huh," I let out.

"Then all the guys could talk about were fag jokes. Mid-scene, the girl had to use the bathroom. So we were all jerking off in a room together. The crew was there. None of them were women. They kept up with the jokes. A bunch of guys making fun of faggots while jerking off together. It was unreal."

"Listen," I tell Joseph. "Don't take it personally. There's no intellectual criteria to do this job. I mean, I like some porn people. But a lot of them are idiots."

"It didn't bother me much. Well...maybe in the beginning," he admits. "There was a lot of time to get myself in the right head-space though. There being six guys. It took the pressure off getting hard right away."

"A lot of things about porn don't make sense," I say. "I haven't thought about it for a while. But I think—in the beginning—I imagined the industry as a sexual utopia. As if everyone were super open-minded. I'm not even open-minded anymore."

"What?" he says. A bit sarcastic. "You make fag jokes, too?"

"Um, no. But I'll laugh at them in a room full of porn dudes."

"You're weird." He laughs.

"Hey, I am open-minded. I can find that shit funny and still get fucked by you."

"I think it's funny. But maybe not for the same reasons."

To put his mind somewhere else (and mine too), I go,"You think you can do this job without me from now on?"

"We'll see."

98.

WE'RE ALL NEW TO STUDIO recording, so we decide to cut a single first. To see how it goes. Also, our bank accounts are better off than usual, but not by much. One song is all we can afford.

Joseph and Thad decide on a track I originally composed. Though it's different now. Has a bunch of parts I've never heard before. They've been writing behind my back. My guitar riffs still flow and it all comes together in the end. I guess it's something I can be proud of.

"What do we do with it now?" I ask.

"Put it on the Internet," says Joseph. "Duh!"

"Send it to labels, too," says Thad. "My friend runs this cool DIY thing that might want to work with us on an EP or full-length."

"Okay, yeah. That sounds awesome," I say. It's the first time I've felt excited about the project in months. "I wonder where this shit might go."

"You never know," says Thad.

99.

OUR SONG IS MET WITH minimal—though positive—response. Someone from a site that calls itself a webzine asks to interview us. We also book our first show with Joseph on vocals.

During the interview, Joseph talks a lot about conspiracy theories and their influence on his lyrics. Although he words it differently: "Those behind the New World Order movement have been implementing their policies for thousands of years. The ultimate goal is to kill off a large portion of the undesirable population. If you view religion as a man-made construct, the apocalypse is not a prophesy. It's a political agenda."

Thad sticks to hardware. "Once I got my hands on this new Roland synthesizer, it all came together. I could be a one-man band with this thing. But the other guys bring so much to the table. So, you know…"

I say something along the lines of, "I've had a recent brush with death and I think it's had a lot of influence on the vibe of this band. Not sure about this song in particular. I'm sure there are other things going on in my head."

Joseph concludes, "I've never played a show in my life. And I never listen to metal. So people should definitely come out to see us. It will be…different."

100.

I'M MOSTLY ASLEEP WHEN JOSEPH goes, "Huh." Loud enough for me to hear and most likely spoken just to get my attention. He spins around in the computer chair until I give in.

"What?" My eyes still shut.

"I got a message from my mom on Facebook."

"Why doesn't she call you?" Even though I don't care.

"She's... I don't know. Scared maybe." Then, "What would you think about going to her place for dinner?" He bites his lip. "Together."

I'm used to fluidity now. Even my hate for Gloria seems possible to put in the past. Though it's not there yet. I should remind Joseph that she probably wants to poison me.

"Oh," I say. "When?" It's a stupid question because the boy lives with me and knows I don't have plans.

"The night after our show. I told her we have to focus on that first."

"It's not that big of a deal," I tell him.

"I have to focus on it," he replies.

"Okay."

"Okay to what?"

"We'll go to your mom's," I say.

Almost immediately, Joseph asks, "What's the deal with your parents?"

My eyes are slits and I haven't actually moved from under the covers. I know he doesn't mean harm, but it's a black hole question. The boy should allow me time to think about it. So I can formulate an answer that doesn't mean anything.

Then right here in bed, I think, *What if this is it and I'm stuck with him for life?* We're supposed to get to know each other. There's always advice flowing in from somewhere about honesty and communication. Of course, most couples are unhappy. The doctrine of communication might be a reason why.

Still, social conduct and our relationship put me in a bind. I have to say something. "Well, they're not dead."

"Who are they? Where do they live?"

"Their names are Barbara and Michael." Most people don't attach meaning to names alone, so I feel like I'm safe. "My mom lives in Northern California. My dad is out in Idaho."

"They're divorced," he assumes.

"Uh huh. Since..." I trail off because I don't actually remember. "It's been a long time."

"What do they do?"

I recall an experience from two years prior. My flight was delayed and I was stuck at the airport with a couple of female porn stars. They got drunk and started talking about their mothers and fathers. Mostly a lack thereof. The moms were both addicts. Neither knew their fathers at all.

It was kind of hot to listen to because I love damaged people. At least fucking them.

Then I felt like I should belong, so I told them how I hated my father. Or used to. He was a binge alcoholic who, after seven marriages, decided he didn't want to die alone. Then he joined AA.

Now he calls me to expound on his sober lifestyle.

I thought it might be inspirational to add that last part. Like my story was a sign of hope. But they just stared at me and shrugged. It was clear that no one gave a shit.

The experience should have been about commiseration and belonging to a sexual clique. Knowing that our parents fucked up provided an excuse to engage in unconventional behavior.

A slut can't help what she does. Because of her father. But I don't need to know the details. And I don't want anyone to know mine. When it comes to sex, I'd rather not have parents. They're irrelevant except to say, "I have a past similar to yours and we should work through it by fucking each other up the ass."

My folks can't compete with Joseph's tragedy and I don't want to make them try. I tell him, "They probably do whatever they want," and add, "You'll meet them some day," with no intentions to make it true.

"I can't wait," says Joseph. "Do you think they'll like me?"

"Who couldn't?"

"You always say the right thing," Joseph tells me before rolling his eyes. "Okay, that's not true. Sometimes you say the right thing."

101.

JOSEPH GETS A LAST MINUTE job on the day of our show. "My agent says it will be quick. No way I can miss the gig." He looks at me to ask if I'll be tagging along.

My answer is, "I need to practice. Haven't played out in a while."

"It'll be the first time by myself," says Joseph. This is followed by a smile. The kind that reaches for confidence but isn't quite sure it's grasped it.

"I love you," I say without affect. I mean it to be reassuring. But it sounds like I don't care.

There's a kiss between us and he disappears out the door.

The practice doesn't happen. I don't even pick up my guitar. However, I think about Joseph in an explicitly physical way. His cock in a girl. It looks nice in my head and I realize I might be able to find this image on the internet now that he's done a handful of scenes.

Tube porn streams past me. I get distracted stroking to some other stuff. Facebook and a few message boards distract me further. I forget I'm jerking off.

Eventually, I close the browser and just stare at the screen. I'm not exactly bored, but I wouldn't know how else to describe it. Then something piques me interest like a spot on a white shirt. I have to take a look and scratch it.

There's a word document on my desktop. Because I haven't typed anything but emails and cam-boy chatter in the past few years, it comes off as unusual. Joseph is the author. Obviously. There's no other explanation. But that's why I have to open it. Even if it's just some lyrics to a song, I should have a right to know. I'm in the band after all.

It's just titled "Draft Six," so I don't get much of a preview. Everything inside is new.

102.

This is hard to write because I feel like I don't know you. I know what you've told me. But that's such an unimportant part of a person.

Whether the opposite is true—whether you know me or not —I can't ignore the fact that you found a way to understand me. I'm not sure how. But you have. You've looked at my skin and peeled it back.

I've been alone most life despite having friends, family, and all the rest. It was worse than being hated. Worse than being forgotten. People would speak to me or touch me like I was a wooden horse or a piece of paper to be drawn on. They would say, "You are this thing," and I'd look inside myself to find it. The thing was never there.

You've looked inside me and found the things I didn't know existed. I cried and sat there, trying to figure out how I felt. What I felt about you. Hours later, when I was all dried up, I could say it was love.

I love you because my soul is reflected in your words. Without you I would have never grown or understood…

103.

THE DOCUMENT GOES ON FOR several paragraphs more, but I close it there. Because I hear the front door open and feet shuffle around the kitchen. Loudly. I don't know what it is about Joseph, but he needs to make his presence clear.

I don't know what it is about Joseph that makes him do most things. It's why I'm confused by his letter. But I put aside his dissent from logic and smile. Focus on the warmth in my chest.

No one's written me a love letter before. I almost believed I'd grown too old and missed out on the part of life when people found them cute, or even necessary. Now it seems absurd that one must outlive written euphoria.

Should I pounce on him as soon as he enters the room? Or is that too obvious? I haven't even read the whole thing and I want my reaction to be fresh when he decides to give it to me.

It's fresh now. The memory of wanting to kill him becomes almost devastating. It's like I want to apologize for everything and say, "It's okay you broke my nose. I forgive you. In fact, I want to thank you for putting me in my place. I might have killed myself if you didn't come along. If you leave, I might still do it."

I already decided that I love the boy. But it didn't really click that the word meant something outside of sex. Not until now. Of course, sex is still part of it. We would have never met without our cocks. Never made it past the first night without a need to put them in each other.

Now I really want to peel his skin back. To find the soul he thinks I can reflect. If it's there, I want to touch it. To blend it with mine. That desire must be love. Sex is only a path to get there. Probably the only one I have at this point.

Joseph should know about this. We should start the process immediately. Try to figure out how to get inside each other without a knife. I'll even let him talk to me about energy. Sit through a Facebook documentary on mysticism and chakras. Any leads on how to get closer to his *other* heart.

I shut my eyes and imagine myself merging with Joseph. His thoughts pour into me and I can almost predict what he'll say first when he walks into the room.

Except I'm way off.

"Fuck everything," he says and falls face first on to the bed. I think I hear him scream into the mattress.

"What happened?" I ask.

"Nothing," is probably what he says. Though it's hard to understand.

"I kind of don't believe you."

"Fucking leave me alone."

The back of his head seems less opaque. Because I'm still trying to read his thoughts. Words pop into my head, but they're changing. Like I'm ripping petals off a flower, saying, "He loves me, he loves me not."

"I feel like I should, um, help you through this," I tell him. "'Cause I love you. Okay?"

There's a motion that's maybe a shrug. Maybe a shiver or minor Parkinson's thing.

"Just tell me," I say. "Otherwise you're going to be pissed about it all day."

"Fine. You want to know what happened?" The boy turns at least five or six degrees. "Fucking nothing. Like I told you. I went to set, didn't get hard, and sat there like an asshole with a soft cock. Then I came home."

"It's okay." I try to kiss him but he almost hits me.

Joseph's eyes look mean even though they're watery. "Don't," he says flatly.

104.

THE STAGE IS DARK AND not actually a stage. We stand on the floor right next to a bunch of kids. Joseph paces with the microphone.

"This is for everyone out there who does their best every fucking day and the world just gives them shit. For everyone

who wants to fucking end it. I know how you fucking feel."
Joseph screams something indecipherable, which I think is a
song title. He looks at me like I should know what it means.

Thad gets it—I think—and starts playing a song. I come in
on my part. Kids start bobbing their heads. Shit gets heavy and
some of the audience moves with violence. Joseph joins them,
screams, and the aggression escalates.

There are only about fifty kids here. By the end of our set,
most of them are sweaty and someone licks blood off his teeth.

"Fuck you guys. Have a good night." Joseph drops the mic
and there's a squeal. The sound guy runs over and calls him an
asshole.

"I think that went well," says Thad.

"Yeah." I agree.

105.

JOSEPH COMES HOME AND I'M already in bed. He doesn't say
anything. It's the first night since he's moved in that we don't
have sex.

My arm goes around him but the boy feels dead. With
resistance. Like his molecules are magnets and they've switched
their charge. I float around him. Never really touching. Never
getting my words into his ears.

"You're beautiful," I tell him.

He sighs.

I look at my phone to distract me from the loneliness. It
has pictures of Joseph. Smiling, naked, and sometimes asleep.
Most of the videos have my cock next to his mouth. But there's
nothing with us together. At least not with our faces.

It's crushing. I try to remember the good old days. Which I
guess are only a month or so ago. There's nothing to trigger the

memory. I begin to panic because I know how often my brain rewrites its own history. The inside of me starts to hurt.

"You still love me, right?"

Nothing.

I start to masturbate because I don't have anything else to calm me down. Also, I'm hoping Joseph might get over his shit and join in. Instead, he shifts his body away from mine. Cold moves between us.

The orgasm takes forever because I'm so upset. But I've learned to come under any condition. Doesn't necessarily make it good.

My stomach soaks in the semen. Somewhere behind my eyes, a wall of flesh barricades whatever usually comes out.

I need to feel something. And I do. The first traces of loss. Probably stupid. I'm overreacting. Joseph's had a bad day. Someone with his energy can't stay like that for long.

It's just such fucked up timing that I almost believe it's planned. I'd do anything for him. Take a bullet even. Yesterday, I didn't know it. Today, I can't take it back.

"Just open your heart and I'll learn how to save you," I whisper into the air.

Joseph actually responds. "What the fuck does that mean?"

"I feel like I'm dying. Because I don't know what you're thinking and… I feel like you hate me."

The boy gets up, grabs his pillow, and stomps towards the bathroom. Before he shuts himself inside, I hear, "Not everything has to do with you."

106.

I TAKE A PISS WHEN the sun comes up and find Joseph asleep in the bathtub. "Good morning."

He wakes up all normal-like, stretches, and goes, "Hey."

It takes about an hour of wandering around the apartment and sitting in different places before we talk about it. He's the one who has to bring it up because I'm acting like we're married and I'm the fifties housewife.

"Do you still want to go to my mom's tonight?"

"Yes. I mean, do you still want me to?"

Joseph says, "I usually like to say whatever I'm feeling. But it's complicated right now. I can tell you that I'm feeling better and that it's okay if we go to my mom's."

"Can I just say that I'm here for you?"

"You just did."

"I know that we're already supposed to be in love with each other," I say, "but yesterday, I really fell in love with you. Because of something you haven't showed me yet."

"You sound like me," he says. "And that's... I don't know. Maybe it's time for a shift in our alignment."

"What?"

"You're trying to manifest something I haven't even done yet. That's why you're in love with me, right? I'm usually all about that. Except for today. I'm rethinking some ideas."

"What are you talking about?"

"Yesterday—on set—I was manifesting my erection. Nothing happened. I could see it clearly in my head. But in reality, nothing."

"Everyone has bad days," I tell him. "Porn is hard."

"My thoughts about you, about our future... That's why I'm here."

"So it works, right? Manifestation, or whatever?

"I'm not sure," he says. "I want to tell my mom to fuck off and that I love her. But how can I tell her to fuck off if I can't do my job? I might have to move back in with her."

107.

WE'RE ON OUR WAY OUT the door. Joseph has to check the mail because he's looking for a check. He doesn't find it. Only a letter from his father.

"Throw it away. We're gonna be late," I say.

"I want to read it."

"Why?"

"It will take five minutes," he says.

108.

Dear Danny,

I've made a friend here in prison and I've told him about us. Please don't be upset. Without your response, I find myself bursting at the seems. An open ear is quite a luxury and I'm afraid I can't help myself.

My friend's name is Charles. He was a high school English teacher until his proclivities for students placed him here. Nonetheless, he was good at his job. At least as far as I can tell. The man knows about stories and he's pointed out the flaws in mine.

I've been trying to work out the reasons my life has gone so awry. Of course, I'm hung up most on the catastrophe that is you and I. Charles may have uncovered a culprit.

My sex had become a myth and I assigned characters to play the parts. You were my Little Red Riding Hood and I was the wolf. I suppose Joseph was the grandmother, however that doesn't make much sense. That's what Charles pointed out. That none of it made much sense.

A wolf is either an explicit predator or a cunning beast in disguise. You know the old saying? A wolf in sheep's clothing? I thought I was something like that.

You couldn't have known much about me. But Charles pointed out that, whatever you believed me to be, I was not a sheep. You didn't suspect I was grandmother either. I'd shot that girl. How could you look at me as anything harmless?

I argued with Charles and told him that you put up no fight. That you sucked Joseph's cock and listened until I fell ill. He insisted that you must have been afraid. Said that you were coaxed largely against your will. Charles told me it was the same with his students. It's why they let him fuck their asses.

Is it true, Danny? You must at least pity me now, having read so much of my intention. From your vantage point, with your ability to understand more than I. It's your capacity for understanding that I envy most. I care about you dearly. I hope you know that.

Charles insists that I am not evil. I trust the man and believe it must be true. He has great knowledge of these things. I look up to him almost as much as you. So you must know that I am good. Could you respond with that? If nothing else? It would make my days much easier to bear.

If I were evil and truly a wolf, I would have snatched you up instantly. I'd have forced you on my cock or used you for some other purpose. My need would have been clear. Much more than it was, or is now. I'd have been that predator. Or I might have worked my way into your life, nice and snug. You'd have loved me by the time I invited you to my home. Then I'd use you for my sex when you least expected. That is the nature of a beast. But I've done nothing like that.

My goal was never to hurt you. Like I wrote before, I was attempting to recover something of my past. I might have also wanted to discover something new.

I'm just an old man with a complex not suited for my time. That's what Charles says. That we were born too late or too early. He could have married his pupils several hundred years ago and no one would bat an eye. Today, he's a pervert.

I'm a murderer because I can't steady a rifle like I used to. Is that my greatest crime? Sure, I've fucked my son and asked you to put your mouth on him. But who was the victim? Not Joseph. He can't even remember it.

Despite not knowing my role or purpose, you've helped me along all the same. Your talent knows no bounds. Nights when I try to figure it all out, my thoughts of you are the greatest ointment. They're not imaginary projections like the fantasies a young boy might have about his crush. You've put yourself out there so that we—the general "we"—understand what you're capable of. We don't have to imagine. We've seen you work right in front of our eyes.

Even so, I wish I was a wolf. I'd be the cunning kind. The one to win your love. I'd have held you and bathed you, and introduced you to my family. You'd have broken bread with Joseph and Gloria. I'd have taught you to shoot a gun—something I never got around to with my son. You would have been a part of me.

I must settle for our friendship and the hope of your reply.

Your friend and admirer,

Ernest Brown

109.

JOSEPH STARES AT THE PAGE long after I've finished reading it. Maybe he's on round two or three.

"We're going to be late," I remind him.

"Why doesn't he write me?"

"You want him to?" I ask, like it's a bad idea.

"I don't know."

"Well, he wouldn't send the letters here."

"I should ask my mom," says Joseph.

"Um, okay..." Then I quickly change my mind. "You know what? No. I fucking care about you. We should rip up the paper and forget about him. Your dad's no good for either of us."

Joseph kind of laughs at me, says, "What's gotten into you?" and walks out the door.

110.

GLORIA HAS ORDERED FROM A restaurant that specializes in home-cooked meals. It's pot roast, vegetables, and mashed potatoes in cardboard cups.

"I don't usually have time to cook," she says, "so it feels like I've forgotten how. But the sentiment's there. If I thought it would taste good, I'd have prepared it myself."

"You used to make pasta," says Joseph.

"You used to complain about it."

"This is good," I tell her.

She smiles and stares me down. "So..."

"We're great, Mom. Everything's fine."

"I didn't suggest otherwise." She's doing the therapist voice.

"And he's good to me," says Joseph.

"I'm not on the offensive here, baby," says Gloria. "Promise. I've had my time to process things."

"Good."

"I'm still processing," she admits. "But you look…taken care of." Her eyes are back on me. Not so long this time.

I try to give her something to be proud of. "Did he tell you he's in a band?"

"Your band?" Not much pride.

I nod.

"I might have seen something on Facebook," says Gloria. "How's the…" She cuts a piece of meat and chews it. Swallows. "…adult film business?"

Joseph's pause is equal to his mother's. Longer even. I just hope it's not to consider how to throw himself under the bus.

"It's okay," he says, finally.

"People are saying good things," I add. "Joseph's doing really well." With this, I reach over and grab his hand.

"What kind of people?" she asks.

"People in the business," I say. "Directors and stuff."

She doesn't quite respond. But her demeanor's not overtly disapproving. "Joseph, I've contacted your school. They say that if you take your proficiency exam in the next month or two, you can attend city college in the Fall."

"What do you want me to do there?" he asks.

"I know you're having fun. But don't you think it's important to have a plan? For the future?" She exploits me for support. "You agree, don't you? That Joseph should think about his future?"

"Yeah," I say. "Of course."

"I'm always thinking about the future," says Joseph.

"That's all I wanted to hear," responds Gloria. "If you need help getting back on track—academically—I know a great tutor."

"Sure, Mom."

"What do you see ahead of you?" asks Gloria. "I'm curious."

Joseph looks at me. His eyes are blank. He's impossible to read.

"I just want to be happy," says Joseph.

"I'll do everything in my power to make sure that you are," says Gloria.

Joseph fidgets and says something quietly under his breath. When no one responds, he says it louder. "I need money."

Gloria acts like she's not phased, but I'm starting to see through her. When she looks back, it goes both ways. I'm probably more embarrassed than Joseph.

Her words are slow. Methodical. "We can talk about that once you've taken your exam. And enrolled. In the meantime… You're welcome to stay here. I still consider this your home."

"We're not actually having money problems," I say. Not sure why. It makes Joseph sound like a thief. But I need Gloria to believe I'm not sucking the life from her son.

Joseph acts like he's heard no one. "And I want to know if dad's been writing."

"What?" This is from Gloria.

"I think about him sometimes."

Her response takes too long and is almost interrupted by Joseph. "If you need to see someone…talk to someone… I can make a recommendation."

"He's been writing, hasn't he?"

"No."

"He writes Chris all the time," says Joseph. "And I read the letters. I know everything."

"He writes Chris?" Gloria may be good at playing her profession, but the rest of her acting sucks.

"You knew that already."

"What do you mean by 'everything?'"

"I mean, like, that dad fucked me. Everything."

This time she's not acting. Unless I'm out of the loop, Ernest's told no one else.

Gloria's face is mostly normal, but her hands are shaking. My silverware rattles on the table. "What do you mean by that?" she asks.

"Your husband raped me," Joseph says plainly.

The shaking moves up to her lip. "Baby, you need to come home."

"I'm dealing with this pretty well, Mom. But I need you to give me his letters."

"There are no letters," she says. The tears are coming now and she's reaching for her son.

"Mom..."

"Baby, I'm not just saying this because you came out of my belly. You're one of the most precious human beings I have ever known. And you've been hurt so badly. You can't even see it. The decisions you're making now are not good for you. They're not good decisions."

"Mom, this isn't..."

"Listen to me, baby. I haven't always been the best mother. Obviously, I didn't pay attention. Didn't see the signs. I'm so sorry."

"It's okay," says Joseph, trying to stop her.

"No." She jumps back in. "It's not. I wish so badly that I could change the past. But I can't and it breaks my heart. Just know, Joseph, that there is so much potential for your life."

"I know," he says.

Gloria tries to hug Joseph from across the table. She grabs his neck and nearly pulls his face into a plate of food. The embrace is then reworked from a standing position. The wetness of the mother is imprinted on her son, or at least on the fabric of his shoulder.

"I love you, Joseph. I'm not going to give up on you."

"Love you, too, Mom," he says, smothered.

"Trust me on this, okay?"

"Okay," says Joseph. Then, "On what?"

"You're going to get all the help you need. But you have to stop this." She looks him the eyes. A mother's will, her love, and most sincere advice: "You can't keep on the way you are or you'll end up like your father."

Joseph pushes her away. "Fuck. Are you serious?"

"Baby..." She reaches for him but grasps only air.

"I kind of don't need this right now," Joseph shouts.

"I know you believe that you like this young man," says Gloria, "but he's damaged goods. Think about it. He's gotten you into pornography...and who knows what else."

"Um, I'm still here," I say to remind her.

"Mom, I wanted to ask you for help," says Joseph. "But seriously... Fuck off!"

111.

THE RIDE HOME IS TENSE and mostly silent. I try to change it up and break the mood. It's not intentional, but I think my attempt is an exquisite corpse. A bunch of lines I've heard from movies. I guess romantic comedies, though I don't watch much of those. So I'm not even sure where they come from. Just that I've heard them before. Spoken by an actor as a scripted way to sound reassuring. They get the job done in my head. But Joseph tells me, "Not now," and later, "Please shut up."

Back at the apartment, I crawl in to bed alone. Again. Joseph sits at the computer for hours while I try to fall asleep. A quiet boy and his glowing screen.

112.

JOSEPH'S BESIDE ME WHEN I wake up. He actually looks at me and smiles.

"I'm sorry," he says.

"Whoa," I reply. "I mean, that's cool. Whatever. You've been stressed."

"I found some article last night on Facebook. It was all about pharmaceuticals. I ended up reading about the side-effects of Viagra. Did you know you can die from that shit? Or have a heart attack, or go deaf. I read that liver failure is common with all prescription pills."

"Common?" It's a lot to take in first thing in the morning.

"It happens," says Joseph.

"Crazy."

"I was thinking, 'Why have I been so upset?' Obviously, my whole belief system's been compromised. But I had to reexamine the context, take everything into account. How can I manifest something positive when I'm putting that shit in my body? The universe knows I'm trying to kill myself."

I'm not really sure what he's talking about, but I say, "I, um, don't think that's true."

"It's like law of attraction. Failure is a form of death. I didn't even know I wanted it. But some things exist outside our consciousness, you know?"

"I don't want to die," I tell him. "And I eat a lot of Viagra."

"That's your choice," he says. "But I can't do it anymore."

"So, what? You're not going to work?"

"I've decided that I really want to be a porn star," he says. "That means I'm going to work. That means I'm channeling a new kind of energy... Fuck my mom. All I can think about is the future, and it doesn't include school or demoralizing parents."

"I'm so in love with you," I say, and try to cuddle him to death—in a purely figure-of-speech kind of way. As an afterthought: "You should look into some of those herbal boner vitamins."

"Particles react differently under observation. We're all just a bunch of mass until someone gives us meaning. I just think that I should be that someone—at least when it comes to my body. A hard cock is an important part of what I want to manifest."

"Where are you getting this?" I ask.

"You don't really pay attention to the Internet, huh?"

113.

JOSEPH GOES TO WORK AND I go shopping. The intention is to buy him something. I figure he deserves a gift for brightening my day.

Unique is on my mind, but I'm not sure what kind. I drive through my neighborhood, past a bunch of signs made out in Korean. To myself: "I wonder what's in all those shops." It's too much effort to find out. So I end up at a sort-of outdoor mall called The Grove.

There's a book store, but I'm pretty sure Joseph doesn't read anything on paper. All the other shops just sells clothes, or things to accessorize them.

I think about stealing an outfit, but I don't know Joseph's size. I'm also really bad at breaking the law. It's a lot like lying. I just can't make it happen without being called out. Not that Joseph's prone to deception because he can shoplift like a pro. The boy's just spontaneous. On my own, I lack anything that could be called exciting or dangerous.

What am I to Joseph? I need to figure out a symbol that transfer to a piece of merchandise. Maybe something to represent the future. That could probably keep us together.

Underwear is not the future, but I spend a lot of time looking at the models on the packaging. Joseph's cock could probably fill out the fabric better than most these guys. Even though their abs are more appealing. But that means the men are either injecting steroids in their ass, or getting help from pixel manipulation and good lighting.

"Fuck it," I say, and grab a pair. Not everything needs to be a metaphor.

I'm still browsing for something extra when I get a call. I answer on the first ring without even looking. Because I'm thinking of Joseph and all the meta shit he talks about. Believing my thoughts into existence.

"Hey pornstar," I say all slutty-like.

"It's Gloria." She sounds annoyed.

"Shit. Sorry."

"Listen, I don't want to waste your time," she says.

"Um, okay."

"I'm aware that you don't like me, and that I've been...less-than-approving of your influence on Joseph."

I'm trying to stay positive and not even get to the awkward part. "You don't even have to... I forgive you. But I think this conversation should be between you and him."

"Wait," she says. "I'm not apologizing. Well, maybe for the way I've gone about it so far." Pause. "I'm sorry."

"For how you've gone about...," I'm about to break the positivity. Then I get distracted by some pictures of models wearing other clothes I think would look good on Joseph. "I'm kind of in the middle of something. Can we talk later?"

"Please don't hang up. I'll be quick."

I look around the store as if someone might help me.

"Do you think...?" Gloria starts again. "How do I say this? Okay. It is my opinion, and also an objective statement, that you could benefit from some self-awareness. Given the situation. And all you've been through."

"I think I'm aware of myself. And I'm also pretty aware of everything that's happened."

"I know. You're a smart kid. But there are things we could all use help with. I'm offering to pay for help...for you...if you're willing to do the right thing."

"Gloria, what the fuck are you talking about?"

"Right. Quick... I'm willing to pay for psychiatric treatment. For you. For a full year. Longer, if you need it. In exchange for..."

"What?"

"In exchange for breaking up with Joseph. I don't want you to talk to him."

"Um, no!" A fellow shopper looks at me, frightened, and shuffles away. I lower my voice and say it again. "No. Maybe you don't get it, but I'm actually in love with Joseph."

"I'm not saying this to attack you, but have you considered the possibility that you're compensating for the lack of power you felt as a victim? I mean with Ernest, and perhaps when you were younger…when you were abused."

"I wasn't abused."

"You don't have to talk about it with me. I understand. Just realize that this isn't all about you. Your actions effect other people."

"If you're talking about Joseph—which, of course, you are—then you should know that I am a great influence." My side of the store is now barren. Someone on the other end looks to be chatting with a security guard, and pointing at me.

"I didn't want to bring it up, but you're making it difficult not to," says Gloria. "That girl, the friend of yours who died… She didn't know Ernest, right? I read that she was an innocent bystander. I'm not saying it was your fault. But what you do is dangerous. People around you can get hurt."

"Hurt by your fucking family. What does that say about the effect *you* have on people?"

Someone puts a hand on my shoulder. His voice means business. "Sir, I need to ask you to leave."

"Wait." To the security guard: "I haven't paid yet." To Gloria: "Give it a break, you know? Just let us be happy."

"I am his mother, and you have no idea the love I am capable of."

"Now," says the security guard.

"I'm getting kicked out of this store. So, um, bye."

114.

Joseph's on the computer, which means he's home from work.

I stand by the door and unhinge myself. Maybe for the first time. I can't remember. Before this, my thoughts were impossible to deal with, and too stupid to say out loud. Now I feel safe enough to open up, or whatever. I mean, only to Joseph.

"You looked so happy this morning and it made me feel really good about myself, and our life together. So I went out to buy you something special. There was this pair of underwear you would have looked really hot in. But your mom called and I got upset. I was kicked out of the store. And I'm sorry, but I really need to vent."

Joseph doesn't look at me. "There's something still out there. Some kind of energy. It's still fucking things up."

"I'm confused," I tell him.

"It's not the Viagra."

"Joseph, I don't know what you're talking about. But can we lay in bed together?"

"Sure," he says, and spoons me on the mattress. He speaks softly in my ear. "I failed again at work. It took me an hour of searching the Internet to find the right information. To calm me down and set me on the right path."

"You're not upset about it?" I ask, and stroke his hair.

"Not anymore. What's the point of being upset?"

"I love your point of view, even though I'm bad at living it. Like, I'm still upset. But this feels good enough to forget about it."

"We have a lot working against us," says Joseph. "The thing that brought us together… He's some of what's keeping us apart. He could even be most of it."

"You mean your dad?"

"I sent him a letter today. It's supposed to be from you."

"What did it say?" I ask.

"It was basically an emotional come-on," he tells me. "I don't know. I wrote about eight drafts before it made sense. They're all on the laptop."

"Eight drafts? What did you call them?"

"I don't understand the question."

"What did you label the files?"

"If you're going to read it, then look at the last one," says Joseph. "It's just called 'Draft 8.'"

"Were you writing anything else?" I ask.

"Don't be angry," he says, and holds me tighter. "Let's talk about your day. What happened with my mom?"

My reason for loving him has to be something more now. There was no love letter. Only eight drafts of fiction.

"I feel sick," I say to Joseph.

"Christopher, she can't hurt you. Not unless you let her. She's not evil like my dad."

"She's not hurting me," I cry out, or whisper. It feels like he's trying to kill me. Like he set me up to misunderstand. My poor heart is breaking. But Joseph's still wrapped around me and he hasn't even lied. There's no way to blame him.

"I have an idea," he says, "to help me out and get your mind off this."

"Can you read me the letter?" I ask. If I hear the words from Joseph, I can still imagine they're for me. It's what I've been waiting for; almost a promise.

"Maybe later. I don't think Ernest should be with us right now. Not even in our thoughts. Look how much it's fucking us up."

The shivering makes me pull him closer. A layer of sweat grows between our skin. The more we come together, the colder I get.

"I was doing laundry the other day," says Joseph. "I came across the red dress in one of your drawers."

"We're not supposed to think about him. You just said so."

"The dress is just a mass of micro-particles until we give it meaning," says Joseph. "Change the way you think about it."

"It still has your come on it," I tell him.

"Could you wear it for me?"

"If that's what you want." Because I need him to think better of me so that he might reconsider what it is I've placed in his head.

"I want to fuck you in the dress." As he gropes at my ass.

Joseph abandons me long enough to rifle through the closet and my personal drawers. He finds the wrinkled dress and hangs it below his neck; poses as if I were a mirror. "I know it looks better on you."

I get inside the outfit and Joseph bends me over the bed. No underwear. The dress frames my ass like a portrait.

"Can you hide your cock?" he asks. "Pull it up or something. So that I can pretend you're a girl."

"Why?" My voice is sad because it's the way I feel.

"Please. I need to know that I can do this."

Joseph rubs his cock around my hole for several minutes. It never fully hardens. He can't even push it in.

"Fuck, I can't get him out of my head." I think he's crying. "Nothing's going to change until I kill Ernest."

I parrot him: "Think about it differently." And then, "You're scaring me."

Joseph crashes on the mattress and hides his face. His words come out fast and muffled. "Before you came home, I read a blog about psychic vampires."

"I don't even know what that is."

"People who are emotionally or psychologically weak... They have to prey on the life force of others. It's obvious this is happening with Ernest and me. Probably with you, too. The blog said you have to remove yourself from the situation. So the vampire can't drain your energy."

My hand tugs on his arm. If I was a child, he'd be my mother's skirt. "Rip up the letters. Please."

"We're already removed and it isn't working. The blog said that if you can't escape the vampire, you have to destroy him."

Still tugging his arm, "You're making that up."

"I have to kill Ernest. Sooner than I thought."

"Shut up," I tell him, and rise above the boy. I stroke with one hand and push the other over his face. It's the same move from when I speed-fuck his hole. But I'm still working it up, not quite hard.

Joseph rolls on to his back and flails his arms to the side. He's not trying to escape, so I'm not sure what's happening.

"Where's my phone?" he asks.

"Shut up," I grunt. My cock is almost ready.

He maneuvers his body to grasp the plastic hidden somewhere in our bedding. The thing comes to life as he mashes it. His eyes peek out between the slits of my fingers. "You look so fucking hot," whispers Joseph. His phone flashes and snaps a picture.

I push my cock in and rock my hips; pull the dress up so I can watch myself buried and resurrected.

"Fuck me," he groans. "Take my ass, Daddy." He says the word over and over. "Daddy."

I hit him everywhere I can.

115.

NOT SURE HOW LONG I'VE been out, but the room is bright. The lights are out. It smells good: Joseph plus something else. A new cologne maybe.

He's standing near the bathroom and throwing on a polo shirt that must be stolen. "We have another show a week from Monday." The boy doesn't ask if I can make it.

"Where are you going?" I ask.

"To work."

"Do you want me to come? I can help."

"I don't think it's a good idea. You've still got Ernest surging through you."

It makes me feel like shit, but an argument isn't worth it. The point would only be to rebuild my self-esteem out loud. Except I'd have to fight with Joseph. I'd almost certainly lose. It's a choice between terrible and worse.

"Have a good day," I tell him.

"Thanks," he says, and smiles.

116.

I CLOSE MY EYES AND wait. The point is to discover Joseph's words as truth, or to come to terms with his mind as either gullible or chronically disingenuous.

What if the boy's right and his father's taken hold of my non-corporeal self? I'd have to feel Ernest after lying still long enough. With all distractions gone, I'd sense that fucking demon. I've spent twenty-five years inside my own head. I better know the difference between my thoughts and the man who killed my friend.

The stuff behind my eyes is typical. There's blackness mixed with fractal patterns, and slivers of light when I grow anxious and almost blink. Then Joseph enters in whatever way is possible. It's not like I see his body or pictures of his face. I just feel his presence. Like energy, or whatever he always talks about.

Joseph's there, and then I'm tired. When he's gone, I can barely stand up. I feel the void I've been searching for. But there's no sign of Ernest. Only a feeling like there's less of myself.

If I could touch that space, I'd imagine it a wound. The kind I might get from sleeping in the forest and allowing the beasts to feed on my flesh.

117.

I GET A LAST MINUTE scene and have to lose the bad mood. It's for a company I've never worked for. They seem to be taking over the world when it comes to porn.

The director says to be on set in an hour. Then he calls back. "Make that two. This girl is really screwing us over."

She's still in makeup when I arrive. No one suggests that I talk to her. This guy, Brandon, who I'm supposed to be double-penetrating her with, tells me she's not that bad. "She's crazy, but I like crazy."

"Don't get me wrong," adds the director. "Once the cocks come out, she's a monster. It's getting her to set that's the problem."

Another hour goes by and the producer orders lunch. We snack on barbeque meats and side dishes. Not that bad. A free meal even if we have to cancel the day.

Then I spot her in the hallway: hooker lashes, red lips, and a black latex outfit that ends at the top of her thighs. She looks like a better version of every other porn girl; if better means augmented for sex appeal.

Because of the context, I feel like I'm staring at a unicorn. It's special because I'll probably get to put my cock in her.

She disappears and rematerializes in the room performers use to hang out.

"Hey, I'm Danny," I say with an outstretched hand.

The girl has a biscuit in her mouth, which she chomps on like a gorilla. It falls into her purse when she notices me. Teeth still chomping, she reaches into the purse and grabs a chunk of bread. It comes apart in her fingers and she rubs the crumbs on my crotch. Then she runs out of the room.

"What the fuck was that?" I say to anyone who will answer.

Brandon laughs. "Today's going to be fun."

"Drugs, right? I mean, what is she on?"

"I don't know. I think that's just the way she is."

"No way. Not possible."

When we get to the stills, she walks down the hall and trips. She's on the floor, crying.

"Are you okay?" asks the director.

"Oh yeah. I'm just kidding," she says, stands, and wobbles. The crying has stopped, or never really happened.

She seems to basically understand what's going on during the introductory acting sequence. But we can never repeat the same performance for different angles. The girl's all over the place.

Finally, we're about to fuck. She goes, "Can I have a quick smoke break? I'm really ADD."

"Fifteen minutes," says the director.

Another hour goes by. I'm still rubbing my cock through my jeans. "What's the status?" I ask.

"She's outside, crying. We can't get her off the phone. I think she's trying to get someone to wire her money."

"Oh my god."

"She asked me if she could use my credit card to buy her a plane ticket. Says her bank account is frozen."

"Is this legal?" I ask. "I mean, because she's really fucking high."

There are shrugs around the room. The director says, "Corporate really wants this scene," as he walks away. His shoulders are all about defeat.

Somehow our cocks are back out and hard before the sun sets. We fuck the girl for a while. It's kind of scary. She wanders off in-between positions and sometimes threatens to kill us.

Towards the end, she goes, "Ow. No, I can't." It's while Brandon is trying to shove his cock in her ass.

"This is a DP scene," says the director. "We have to get in another DP position."

"It's not worth it," she says. "My ass is gonna tear apart."

"Do you want to cancel the scene, or do you want to keep going?" asks Brandon.

I'm praying—or I guess hoping—for the first one.

"We're almost done," says the director.

"Because you just said that," she stammers, "I'm gonna keep on going." I don't think her eyes are even open.

Brandon tries to fuck her ass again, but she stops him. "Ow. It's not your cock… I think it's the lube."

"What do you want us to do?"

"Pour water on it," she says.

It's the first time I take initiative. I find a bottle and rinse her gaping hole. "Is that good?"

"Get a towel," she says. The second time it's shouted. "Get a towel!"

Someone does, and she places it beneath her.

"Now what?"

"I'm shitting!" she screams. "I'm going to fucking shit."

"Is she serious?" I ask.

Brandon goes, "Of course not," and laughs.

I'm not sure why I can't decide on the right thing to do. It should be obvious. No one needs the money that bad. Maybe the girl, but I can't tell for sure. The way she looks, the price of her clothing and bags; it means someone's supporting her. Unless the crash was sudden and steep. I can imagine her dying within the year. In a way, it's kind of hot.

The director says that he'll never hire her again, and neither will the company. I'm a part of the end. So I stick my cock back in her.

When I'm supposed to come, she looks sincere. "I want it," she says with pleading eyes. "Give it to me."

118.

JOSEPH STANDS IN THE KITCHEN and sips some sort of smoothie. "How was your day?" he asks, nonchalant.

"Not that good."

"Why?"

"Because I had a job and it was really fucking stressful." I'd usually say this while moving towards him, getting all close. Today, I'm not sure if I'll be pushed away.

"Did you come?" he asks.

It's a weird question. "That's almost the point of porn." When there's silence, I add, "Yes."

He shrugs. "Then it couldn't have been that bad."

"Did you come?"

"Yes."

"So everything went fine?" My voice sounds condescending. I guess on purpose. "You're happy again?"

He shrugs once more. "Do you want to get some dinner, or something?"

119.

I HAVEN'T TOUCHED MY THAI noodles because I'm tired and Joseph's telling me a bedtime story. "When this is all over and we've made our fortune, I want to start a commune. Maybe buy a villa in France. We'll have lots of land. All the people I've met and loved in my life can come and stay for free. They can grow their own food and make their own clothes. We can even sell things like the Zapatista women in Chiapas.

"You and I will have the biggest room. It will be the future, so our garden will be inside. We can grow spinach and tomatoes. Even kale so I can get better at making it taste good.

"My mom will grow old there. She won't be upset anymore because we'll have done so well. She'll see that we're successful. The air will be pure. She'll live longer. At ninety-years-old, she can go for walks in the forest.

"You can entertain the guests with your music. And do whatever else you want." He takes a bite of some curry dish, and looks up and down my face. "You'll be so handsome when you're older. I can't wait to see it."

I close my eyes, but can picture none of it. "When did you come up with this?"

"I've thought about it forever. Mostly in my dreams."

"You've just brought it up now."

"We don't know each other," says Joseph. "Not really. I hate that you don't tell me things."

"What do you mean? I tell you things."

"Not about your dreams."

"I don't remember my dreams. And if you mean my thoughts about the future, I can't think that far ahead."

"What about this week?" he asks.

"I don't know. Might have a couple of jobs. We probably have to practice with Thad."

"Oh…"

I can tell he wants me to ask. "What do you want to do?"

"My agent says I should take some time off. You know, get my head together… I think I'll do that."

120.

I'M BOOKED THE NEXT FEW days. Joseph leaves the apartment before I go to work. Sometimes he's back when I return. Sometimes not.

His eyes are dreamy when I see him, like he's asleep or dead. I can't point out what's wrong. He eats, speaks, and allows me to fuck him. But his eyes look the same when I tell him how much I love his ass, and when I hold his face after.

"I wish you could see inside my head," says Joseph. "It would be so much easier."

"You can tell me what's there. I want to know."

"That's the problem with words."

"Where do you go when I'm at work?" I ask.

"On walks mostly. To think. To try and put things together." He stares off. Somewhere far away. Through the wall, I guess.

There's no window. "It might have the opposite effect." Eyes back to me. "But I'm happy. I'm looking forward."

It turns into a kiss. One that's full and slow. Not like when we first met. Still, it feels young. As if Joseph's right. There's something to look forward to.

121.

I ARRIVE HOME FROM MY last scene of the week. The apartment is empty and the mailbox full. There's a letter I don't want to open. I lock myself in the bathroom and read it anyway.

122.

Dear Danny,

I've been crying all day. I'm crying now. Believe me, they're tears of joy.

Mere acceptance is what I hoped for. I prayed even. Though at the time, I didn't understand what to. I should have known who heard me. The devotion you arouse confirms your godliness. All those nights I called out, there was no void. Only you.

I've been scared of God my entire life. I could never believe the books that said He loved me. What man of little faith I am.

To read that you love me, that you can see inside my heart and understand it; oh Danny, what can I say to that? Only that you are my everything now.

I hurt because you have hurt. So much it seems from the looks of your letter. I wish to take on more of your burden. If possible, I'd take it all.

To read, in your own words, how I helped sooth you; I'm humbled more than I can say. It opens my heart and mind. I must acknowledge that we are part of some greater plan. We've come together under such extraordinary, dare I say divine, circumstances.

Of course, earthly efforts have been made. I understand you more than most because I've taken the time to do so. It's been several years now. Like an angel, I've watched over you. Since shortly after your pornographic birth.

Looking back, did you feel my presence? Something inexplicable resting on your shoulder? I have so much to ask you, so much to learn about our connection. Together, we must do our part to understand.

You'll come and visit, won't you? I've no greater excitement than to see you in the flesh. Danny, you must know I yearn to hold you. A shake of your hand would be enough. My heart is overwhelmed, bursting even. Because it's heard my eyes, and they know you feel the same as I do.

The guards tell me Monday is best to visit. Between three o'clock and five. I trust this letter will find you soon and bring you back to me.

With all the love I have,

Your Ernest Brown

123.

JOSEPH'S RETURNED. I CAN HEAR him.

"Just a minute!" I shout from inside the bathroom. It must sound suspicious. I have no reason to believe he's sought me out.

The letter should be disposed of. My first thought is in the toilet. But I recall the signs posted above porn-rental-house porcelain: *"Do not flush feminine products or baby wipes. Toilet paper only."*

Ernest's letter isn't feminine or infant-like, but I'd rather not chance it. I don't need to be reminded of the asshole while cleaning our overflow of shit.

What else is there? No adhesive in the room, or else I'd tape it under the tank lid. I fold the letter ten times and hide it in the mirror cabinet. Beneath a tube of hair product.

I flush to continue my charade, and open the door. Then rub my stomach as if I've had a bad meal.

Joseph doesn't notice. He says, "I want to show you something."

124.

WE WALK A MILE. MAYBE more. Through a part of town like all the rest.

Joseph leads me over a fence and through a door that should be boarded up. Inside, light falls from the broken ceiling. It's as if the structure glows.

"I found it today," says Joseph. He holds a hand to his chest and turns in circles. "Isn't it beautiful?"

The walls are cracked and full of graffiti. In the corner, there's a weathered couch and a mattress that someone probably died on. If I imagine myself as a high school photographer, I can sort of see the appeal.

"Yeah, it's cool," I tell him.

"This place gave me an idea. What if we say, 'Fuck it?' Fuck the porn establishment. They tell us what sex should be like. It's basically set up for us to fail. But if we make our own..." Joseph holds my hand like he's about to propose. "If we show people what sex can be...what it really is..."

The boy drops to his knees and says, "Take out your phone."

It's the look in his eyes and the way he bites his lip. The promise that continues with a ripped-open belt. Blood flows and I begin to thicken. No choice but to obey him.

Joseph comes to life in the center of my smart-phone. His mouth opens and consumes me whole.

Between gasps and gags of flesh buried in his throat, Joseph says, "Film me like an artist. I want to know how our sex looks when you've painted me as 'beautiful.'"

I'm not sure what he means, but I gather more close-ups than usual. I fixate on his lips and my cock dragged across his tongue.

The camera's focus flutters, and I capture a moment of dust reflected in the light. It reminds me how dirty this place is. Maybe that's what Joseph's looking for. To show the filthy side of him: in focus and lit-up. It sounds like all porn. There must be a trick to getting something more.

The friction picks up and I explode in his mouth. He holds it open for the digital memory. So my cum can be preserved in detail. Then he stands and gives me his lips. Delivers back my seed.

We cuddle together in the abandoned building and watch the act on repeat.

"So hot," says Joseph. "In a place like this, it feels more real."

"I kind of see what you mean," I say. "You look like sex incarnate. But I'm not sure what you want to do with this."

"Don't you think it's weird we have to hide? No one in the industry knows we're together."

This is the first time he's brought it up. In the beginning, I didn't want the label. Now it's a necessity to keep it under wraps.

"You know the reason why," I say. "No one would hire us. Fags are blacklisted. We'd be fucked."

"Unless no one had to...hire us."

"Joseph, this is cool, but it's not a movie," I remind him. "We don't have distribution. And I don't even know anyone in gay porn who could help us find it."

"Why does it have to be 'gay porn?'" He does the quote thing with his fingers.

"Because we're two guys fucking each other. When you film it, that's gay porn."

"Okay, but we're doing something different," he says. "Besides, we have to think about the future."

His excitement doesn't quite latch on this time. But I guess porn production is my inevitable gig, post-performing. In the meantime, what could it hurt to film ourselves every once in a while? We could always keep it private until it no longer matters.

"If you want to shoot porn, I'm game. I just don't think we should tell people until we know it can make money."

He hugs me and gets all fired up. The force inside him makes the boy want to jump. "Totally! We'll play it cool for a while. Then blindside everyone. They won't even know what happened!"

We walk hand-in-hand most of the way home. Until Joseph finds something up ahead that allows him to detach. He calls it, "Beauty in the world," and can't bring himself to be more specific.

His body shrinks in my vision and I let go of my smile. I wish he'd share his secret, or feed me the stuff that makes him glow.

Amidst our last hundred yards, Joseph turns towards me and bites the air with his mouth. I don't feel his teeth. But there's a space behind my skin where they might as well have left their mark.

125.

WHEN WE'RE AT THE APARTMENT, Joseph says, "The agency called and asked if I can go back to work. I think I'm ready, so I told them, 'Yes.'"

"That's good to hear," I say. "I'm happy for you."

"I have a job on Monday. Do you think I can borrow a Viagra?"

I'm amused. "What made you change your mind?"

"I read a Facebook post about white privilege and the necessity to cheat. It's in our DNA." There's no way to tell if he's joking. "Besides I need money to invest in our porno. And money for the commune. The universe will see the bigger picture and forgive my self-abuse."

I have to smile and say, "Okay." Then I dig around in my stash. "You're crazy. You know that?"

"How come?" he asks. "I mean, I'm not."

Two blue pills fall from my hand into his. "You have to buy them after this. Porn boners don't work on miracles."

"Don't forget," he says. "You and me… We're a miracle."

126.

SUNDAY IS SPENT IN BED together. We order takeout: Thai, Chinese, and then pizza. There's no sex except for jerking each other off—lazily—and laughing about it.

I make Joseph watch a foreign film about a low-level mobster who's testicles are crushed as a child. Failed masculinity is replaced by testosterone injections, lifting, and violence.

Joseph makes me watch an online "documentary" called *Thrive*. It's every conspiracy theory rolled into one—narrated by the heir to Procter & Gamble. Because there's mention of aliens, and I'm casually into sci-fi, I give it a chance. But it seems like antitax propaganda from a guy who has too much money.

We discuss why Joseph thinks the movie makes sense. After, he says, "I have to go sleep. Big day tomorrow. There's work and then our show."

"Can I give you a massage?" I ask.

The boy coos and rolls on to his stomach. A better form of yes. I mount his lower back and push my hands into his shoulders. Manipulate him to sleep. His breath begins to slow and the muscles in his face relax. He looks goofy in a way that only lovers find cute.

I snap a few photos with my phone. Text the best one to Joseph. It's objectively creepy, but I know he likes it when we watch each other sleep.

Along with the picture, I send a note: *"If I dont c u in the morning...wreck that pussy for me. <3"*

127.

THE SOUNDS ARE TYPICAL OF when I'm the last to wake: running water, microwave beeps, a flush, and footsteps. I keep my eyes closed even when my brain starts to pick things up—consciously. Training wheels for a new day.

My bladder won't allow the daze its due time. So I'm up and knocking at the bathroom door.

The response is delayed. Joseph comes out a minute later and gives me the look of death.

"What?" I'm totally thrown off. "What did I do?"

He doesn't speak to me. Just picks up his phone and dials. I can barely hear the ring on the other end. When the voice comes, I can't understand it at all.

"Hey, it's Joseph," he tells the phone. "Sorry, but I have to cancel my scene." There's fury on the other end. That much is clear. "It's personal." Then, "What? I know it's last minute... yeah. Uh huh...an emergency...Yeah, I said it's an emergency." He starts to yell. "Because I can't fucking deal with this right now!"

I leave the boy to sort it out. Take my piss with the door closed behind me. That's when I spot Ernest's letter—unfolded— wet in the sink. The rest of my urine hits the floor.

"What would be a good excuse?" shouts Joseph when I'm back in the same room. "Okay, you got me. That's the reason. I have fucking HIV!"

He hangs up and burns a hole through me. At least that's what it feels like.

"Why did you say that?" I ask. Because Joseph might have just fucked up his career.

"You're a liar," is the only answer I get.

He paces and gathers some things. I can't even tell what they are until he's grabbing my car keys.

"Where are you going?" I ask. He heads for the front door and I grab him. "You're not going where I think you're going."

"I wrote the letter. I got the response. It's not your place to interfere."

"Fuck you!" I push the boy back into our home. "I thought that letter was for me."

"What?" He looks offended, or something. "I've been telling you for months that I'm going to kill my dad. And I told you why I wrote him..."

"After," I say. "You told me after!"

"After what?"

"After I read it."

He laughs in the meanest way possible. One short scoff. "You didn't read it very well."

"I read the beginning. It was really sweet and I wanted to wait for the rest. So that when you gave it to me, I'd be surprised." I'm not sure why I'm holding back tears, pretending not to be emotional when I obviously am. "But apparently you're only capable of saying something nice when you're making shit up."

"I love you," says Joseph, "but get the fuck out of my way."

My body doesn't budge until he takes a swing. Then I'm off to the side with my hands up, going, "Fine. Do what you want. But have you even thought about it? You can't kill a man in prison without ending up there yourself!"

128.

THE SOBBING ENGULFS ME AND is otherwise not worth describing. Though it ends without Joseph's return. I text Thad, and follow up with a voicemail. "Joseph took off with my car and I think he's going to do something stupid. I don't know how much you guys talk, but maybe you can stop him."

An hour goes by and I can't remember anything about it. Except that I've been shaking.

Eventually, I sit at the computer and log on to Skype. I guess with hopes to find a friend who still considers me one. The options aren't great, but Thad makes an appearance. I engage him with video chat.

"Why didn't you text me back?"

"Oh," he says, and picks up his cell. "What's wrong?"

It's weird because I don't talk to Thad about anything personal. "You know Joseph's dad is in prison, right?"

He shrugs. "I do now."

"Fuck, I don't even know where to start. Um, Joseph's probably going to try and kill him."

"Who?"

"His dad. He's going to try and kill his dad."

Thad doesn't look worried. "That sounds really hard to do if the guy's in prison."

"I'm not sure. Joseph took my car, and that's basically what he said he'd do."

"Did he say he'd be at the show tonight?"

"We didn't really talk about it."

"I chatted with him a couple days ago," says Thad. "He sounded pretty hyped about the show."

"Yeah, a couple days ago…"

"He's not that stupid. Let's just show up and see what happens."

"But…" I try to express the gravity of the situation, and come up with, "I don't have my car."

"I'll swing by your place if he's not back in time," says Thad. "Don't worry about it. He will be."

"Can you at least call him?"

"Now?"

"He won't answer me."

"Fine." Thad swipes his finger across his cell. A few more times and I can hear the ringing. Except no one picks up. "Don't know what to tell you. I'll try again later."

"Yeah," I say. "Thanks."

129.

I CHECK OUT UNTIL MY laptop makes one of those instant message noises. It's an IM from Thad.

Thad: Have u seen this?

He sends me a link to a *Huffington Post* article. The headline: "Porn Actor Comes Forward As HIV+. Adult Industry Halts Production." There's a picture of Joseph right under it.

Me: Fuck.

Thad: Is this for real?

Me: No.

Thad: It's on *Huffington Post.* Seems real.

Me: I need to get a hold of Joseph.

Thad: Now I'm worried about the show.

I log off and freak out. Just enough to keep my mind from following through. I'm not sure with what. That's kind of the problem.

As far as I know, nothing's changed with Joseph. I don't know how to reach him. Our phones can keep us together and just as easily apart. The boy could be bluffing—anywhere. Or waiting around outside the state prison.

Most people calm down eventually. He probably will, too. If that's what I'm hoping for, I guess I should be the one to start. I search YouTube for yoga videos and breath deeply in my chair.

The poses look difficult to pull off. I don't even try. Instead, I call Joseph and hyperventilate on his voicemail. "Please come home."

Then my phone blows up and I decide to answer. "Hello?"

"Hey, it's Eugene." I've worked for him a couple times. He's a director for Platinum Angel.

"Hey."

"Word is that HIV kid is your friend. You got the scoop?"

"I think it's a misunderstanding," I tell him.

"Yeah? According to what?"

"I, um, don't know if it's my place to say."

"That sounds sketchy, man. If it's a misunderstanding, what do you have to hide?"

"Nothing. I think he said it as a joke."

"That he has HIV?" There's a lot of disbelief.

"Yeah."

"I don't want to start shit, man. But I got this girl who's telling me she did a scene with the kid. She says you were on set. Says you guys went into the bathroom together and he came out with a hard-on. Do I need to say more?"

"I don't have HIV."

"This girl pulled up some pictures of you sucking cock," he says.

"It was a long time ago."

"Maybe so. But the fact remains… Every time this happens, it's one of you crossover guys."

"I already told you it was a joke."

"Be honest, man. I'm just looking for the scoop."

"Okay," I say, and hang up.

130.

THE HOLE I NEED TO crawl in doesn't exist. Not in my apartment. I stay low to the ground like a burrowing creature that's lost its strength to dig.

The red dress is down here with me, crumpled near the bed. Every time I put it on, a piece of my world ends. Then it's discarded. Never lost. It sticks to me and propels my story forward. Each chapter, I'm closer to death.

I don't even know how the Red Riding Hood fairy tale goes. Some bitch is in the forest. There's a lumberjack, grandmother, and wolf. Each character means something. Ernest couldn't explain it to me. With Gloria, we were supposed to figure it out—what it meant in real life. Then our thoughts became violent. Too much to cooperate with each other.

The dress was hers. That's all I can think now. The energy Joseph told me haunts things; it might be Gloria hidden in her clothing. Maybe Red Riding Hood isn't even a person, just a thing. So the wolf might be inhuman, too. Just an idea. Like imaginary HIV.

I try Joseph's trick and view the dress as a mass of uncharged particles. Neither positive or negative. The will inside me wishes them to melt, turn to vapor, and become abstract thought.

It does nothing but sit there and stink. The smell of this world: blood, sweat, and come.

131.

I'M NOT SURE WHEN IT was sent. But there's an IM from Thad waiting for me on the laptop.

Thad: What do u think? Should we go 2 the show?

Me: Maybe you can come and get me. We can figure it out.

Thad: I tried calling again. No answer.

Thad: The HIV thing's on other sites.

He sends me a few more links. The adult industry blogs have even picked it up.

Thad: Does this mean Joseph's gonna die?

Me: It's not real. Trust me.

Thad: I guess I'll see you in…

Thad: 1 hr?

Me: Yes please.

132.

THAD PICKS ME UP AND we drive to the practice spot. To get our gear.

"Maybe we should cancel," says Thad. "I wouldn't want to play a show if I knew I was dying."

"Fine with me."

"On the other hand, maybe it's what I'd want most. Especially if I was a vocalist. I'd need to scream and get it off my chest."

"He's not dying," I say. It feels like the hundredth time. "That's not the real danger."

"How do you know for sure? How are you right and the whole Internet is wrong?"

"Because I know more about him than the Internet. We live together. And I love him." The last part is added because if anything happens to Joseph, I can't bear it alone. Like right now. Everyone keeps telling me he'll be murdered by a virus.

"You love him? How long have you known this guy?"

"We're fucking, Thad."

He doesn't seem shocked. But there's enough for him to furrow his brow. "I…didn't…know that."

"I guess we don't talk much about normal stuff."

"So you don't have HIV?"

"No," I tell him. "I mean, last I checked."

"And the Internet?"

"Joseph made it up so he could get out of work today. Because he's stupid."

"Fuck," says Thad. "That is pretty stupid. Maybe he will kill his dad."

"Do you think he'll show up?" I ask him. "He talks to you more about music stuff."

"I don't know." He puts on his thinking face. "This is crazy. We're basically a homo-core band."

133.

OUR LACK OF ASSERTION MEANS we go with the plan. The one set in motion before we had to decide. Even at load-in, we don't tell the promoter what's going on. Thad agrees to cross our fingers and wait. Three hours to go before things are fixed, or fall apart.

The first band of the night is slow and heavy. Funeral doom. My heart clocks in at pace and I hibernate. One long nod of the head.

Band number two picks up the pace. Some grind parts, but mostly ethereal black metal. It's a perfect sound for the fear inside me. Where my relationship is a void, and my love an abyss. I can at least rest easy on the fact that plenty of Joseph's physical attempts have failed. If murder is at all like erections, the statistics are promising. He should be back here and sulking. The world may move on, unchanged.

But he's not back in time for us to set up the stage. Thad asks, "Do you want to do vocals if Joseph doesn't show? I feel weird backing out this late."

"I don't know the lyrics," I admit.

"You can just scream stuff like you used to." Then after consideration, "Are you okay? I mean because you guys are… whatever you are."

"He's probably still mad at me and doing this on purpose." It means I'm good enough to play. Because Thad pats me on the back and goes off to grab his synth rig.

I stand with my guitar and look out at the dwindling crowd. No longer sure why I'm here. No longer sure why, if the question is anything.

A familiar face walks towards me. I mistake her for someone I like, and smile. She smiles back, larger and more sincere.

Then I get it. Gloria is several feet before me and reaching inside her purse. She pulls out a handgun and waves it near my crotch. A sound comes from her mouth. I can't hear it.

Suddenly, a burst. My ears start to ring. There's wetness near my legs and I feel as if I'm dying.

Other people scream, but not me. I'm on my back and can't breathe.

Gloria crouches and whispers in my ear. "I told you if anything happened to my son…"

The pain is overwhelming now. I can feel her try to get inside me, though the sensation is entirely new. No way to figure out what's happening unless I look. It's what causes the black to overcome me.

Before I pass:

I see a hole in my pants right below the belt. It's large and grows with Gloria's fist. Blood spurts up around her hand and everything becomes the same color.

She digs in the wound where my cock and groin should be. A piece is still there. I can see it pushed to the side.

"Die, you faggot." Her hand disappears to the wrist and I can take no more.

134.

THE SKY IS WHITE ABOVE me and no sky at all. Plaster and paint, and lit like a hospital. No one's here to greet me and I don't have the strength to call out.

I can hear them beyond the wall: doctors, nurses, and staff. After a time, someone stops by to watch me suffer. She's pleasant enough and instructs me how to flood myself with morphine. I do it twice before she leaves the room.

The doctor explains what's wrong. That I've sustained a serious injury. "We've done our best to patch you up," he says. But I will never be the same.

There's enough of a urethra left in my nub to let some piss dribble out. Though things must heal before a catheter is no longer necessary.

"Is there someone we can call?" he asks.

I tell him, "Joseph Brown."

He replies, "Anyone else?"

I cry until he leaves, and for some time after.

135.

THAD COMES A DAY OR two later. Maybe a week. He doesn't say much, but he drives me home.

"I guess the band's over, huh?" Then, "If you need anything… let me know."

My shell is quiet and haunting to look at. I know this because I can see a piece of it reflected in the laptop screen behind Thad. There are no details. Just my black silhouette.

I would leave. The same way Thad leaves. Because I'm like death across the ocean, or on television. Sad to think about. Impossible to fix.

My vision blurs because I've forgotten to blink. "What happened to him?" I ask.

There's no one here to answer.

136.

I'M AT THE COMPUTER NOW. Because of habit.

There are names on Skype I recognize. Most I'd never talk to. Damien's SN is blocked. Probably from the time Joseph broke his heart and I did nothing to stop it.

I unblock him because I need someone to tell me I'm beautiful. Memory says he's the best chance I've got.

Damien shows up online. I don't wait like I used to. He accepts my request for video chat.

"Danny…"

"Hi." I'd be bashful if I could figure it out.

"It's good to see you." He drops his eyes. "I didn't think I would."

"Things have changed," I say. "I've changed."

"What do you mean?"

"The boy is gone."

Damien looks happy and then sad. All in an instant. "I can't pay you."

"It's okay," I tell him, and wish we could touch. Choked up, I ask, "Would you look at me?"

He seems to grow in his chair. His shoulders no longer reach so far to the ground. "I still think about you sometimes."

The swiveling starts. What I used to find so embarrassing in him is now a charm. Damien's excited. I love that he can't hide himself from me. Even when I look like a ghost.

He says, "Yes. I'll look at you any time you want."

"I've changed," I say again. This time as a warning.

To stand is a chore. To remove my pants is worse. I do both, and hope he finds the masochism worthwhile.

"What happened?" he asks when the thing is visible—my bandage and its crust.

I can only shrug. Because I haven't seen myself either. Not since before I was shot. What happened otherwise is not a thing I can explain.

The bandage comes off and I make noises through my teeth. "Don't," says Damien when it's nearly done.

"But you said…"

I don't have to worry. He follows through. Then I take my turn.

There is flesh where some of it should be. Much less than I'm used to. Coarse thread pulls my meat together in shotgun-patterned stitch. All of it is bruised, or else hidden by black coagulation.

"Say something."

He doesn't. Not until I'm seated.

"I'm sorry," says Damien.

"I remember how you said you loved me. And how I treated you so bad." My nose is snotty. I might be pouring if the rest of me weren't so dry.

"You gave me a lot of time to think," he says. "I realized you were right. This thing we have, or had… It's not love. I never loved you."

"It's okay." Even though I feel the opposite.

"I'm sorry things have changed. But it's scary to look at you. I don't think I can."

137.

THERE'S NO NEWS THAT I can find to tell me what's happened. No one at the hospital remembers how I got there, and I don't want to call the police.

Joseph's voicemail is full before I can finish my message. I'm able to record a croak. Days later, when I think to try again, my phone service is shut off. I have nothing left to pay it—to turn it back on.

My message to Thad is simple.

Me: Do you know what happened to Joseph?

Thad: He never called back.

I stare at my butchered nub. It scares me. Like it did with Damien. Worse because I need to touch it.

My hand moves down eventually. Whether I look at the nub or not. My brain responds at first contact. Because the touch is familiar. It was boredom and release. Sometimes my pleasure, too.

I remember most when others put their hand there. When they weren't paid and didn't have to. I stopped caring until Joseph. Until he was halfway done with me.

Before him, and before porn, there were others who touched me. Awkward, slow, and private. I don't remember their names. Only that we built it up so much. My cock could do harm or create life, which I viewed as terrible back then. Still, they would touch it. They didn't care how dangerous it was, how dangerous we were together.

Then I was paid for sex and I found my self-worth. I lost track of everything after.

Until I found the boy and the love inside of him. The stuff that tricked me into believing it was made up or for someone else. I know it's real. Because it stretches my wound. It brings to life what's been cut from me.

My skin begins to split and the stitches break apart. In the moment before it, I can feel him. Joseph wrapped around me. Joseph in my bed. I ask him where he's gone. He says, "I'll always be with you."

Then I'm flayed open. Jerking between my finger and thumb. I can feel Gloria now, and the pain she's gifted me. "I'm here because you took my son," she says, though I've asked her nothing.

"He came to me on his own," I reply.

I keep jerking my nub. With Joseph and Gloria beside me. In spirit, if nothing else.

Enough blood flows to keep me aroused. To balance the pain and keep the puddle from going dry. I must jerk until completion. The wound must spill.

He brought them to me first, so he finds it fair to join us. Ernest knocks at my brain, and we invite him in. Grudgingly. He still calls me a god, and says, "Even gods can lose their limbs."

He says, "I am not a wolf. I did not make you love me, and I did not destroy you. But look at my family. Look at what you've done."

"What did I do?" With Ernest at my ear, I can hardly believe my erection. Until I look down. There's so little of me to keep engorged.

"Everything I asked of you," he says.

I feel the family push themselves on me. They whisper what I should be. Because it's mixed with my sex, I believe them.

My climax grows to its tipping point and I am released from my groin. The spirits in my brain take my place. I can even see past them. To the others who've made me their home.

Sara is in there. In my head. She says that I'm meant for her and cries when I can't tell her, "yes," or, "no."

I say, "I don't know," crawling in the muck of blood and cum that I've left on the floor. "I feel like I used to want you, but I don't know."

"What should I do?" I ask. Not to Sara, Joseph, Ernest, or Gloria. But to all of them.

"You are this thing…" Ernest's voice trails off as my nub falls flaccid. I hate the sound of him even as it leaves. Also, I miss it.

I search for the thing I used to have before: desire—or something like it. If it's there, I can't grab hold.

"Tell me what I should want!" I cry out. "Not for you, but me!"

They've disappeared, so I grab at my cock to bring them back. Because it's not there, I wail. When I see the nub torn off—drowned in my puddle of blood and come—I scream.